I0662691

# Beloved Enemy

## by

## Hywela Lyn

*The Destiny Trilogy, Volume 3*

This is a work of fiction. Names, characters, places, and incidents are either the product of the author's imagination or are used fictitiously, and any resemblance to actual persons living or dead, business establishments, events, or locales, is entirely coincidental.

**Beloved Enemy**

Cover Art by *Rae Monet, Inc. Design*

The Wild Rose Press, Inc.
PO Box 708
Adams Basin, NY 14410-0708
Visit us at www.thewildrosepress.com

Publishing History
First Fantasy Rose Edition, 2016
Print ISBN 978-1-5092-0534-9
Digital ISBN 978-1-5092-0535-6

*The Destiny Trilogy, Volume 3*
Published in the United States of America

**She scrambled to her knees,**
still slightly winded, and fired at the hideous thing. The foliage around it flared briefly with an eerie green flame, and the tentacle shrivelled into a slimy black mass, emitting a pungent odour and causing her to gag.

"It seems I was mistaken about the creature being dead." Kerry prodded the smouldering mass with his boot and looked across over the water. "It is now." He leaned down and grasped her wrist to haul her to her feet. "Are you hurt?"

"No, I don't think so." Her shoulder was sore and probably bruised but she'd live.

She tried to control her shivering. The incident affected her more than she wanted to admit. Kerry's proximity—naked to the waist, his lithe body shining from the water droplets that still clung to his skin, and his legs swathed in tight black leather—did nothing to help. The last thing she wanted was for him to realize how scared she'd been when she thought a snake attacked her.

"Thanks. That was close. It would have been a bit ironic if I'd been killed by the same creature I saved you from."

She realized he still grasped her wrist. She tried to move away, but he pulled her back, obliging her to turn to him.

"You're trembling."

"I'm fine."

"No," he said. "You're not." He pulled her closer and his eyes softened, his gaze holding her mesmerized. She opened her mouth to try to speak, but in the same instant, he put his hand under her chin and his lips closed over hers.

## Praise for Hywela Lyn

"Never judge before you know the facts. [In *BELOVED ENEMY*,] Kerry Marchant is not the villain Cat Kincaid thinks he is…the strange cause of all their troubles is a shock that fills in all the blanks in a satisfying conclusion."

~*Mary Ricksen, Author of Burned Into Time*
~*~

"*STARQUEST* by Hywela Lyn is a sweet and wonderful book…that will keep you on your toes and end with a big smile on your face. An adventure like no other…"

~*Amylove, WRDF Reviews*
~*~

"I must say that *STARQUEST* takes the reader onto an awesome galactic journey. The characters are strong and convincing…One will not find a dull moment with this story; it is loaded with action from beginning to end…Hywela Lyn weaves a romance that is truly out of this world."

~*Cherokee, Reviewer for Coffee Time Romance*
~*~

"Hywela Lyn creates a very vivid and wonderful world in *CHILDREN OF THE MIST*. Her characters have depth beyond any I have seen in a science fiction novel. She has the ability to give them souls in the literary sense, which is a rare talent. The extensive descriptions of the world she has created forms in the mind almost like the memory of a place once visited…It was a journey well worth taking and…I look forward to reading more books by this author."

~*Marilyn Thompson, Mind Fog Reviews*

## Dedications

For my dear friends and fellow writers, especially my crit partners: Mary Ricksen, my "soul sister across the pond" and Echo Shea, Sarah Tranter, and Miss Mae for their help, advice, and support.
For my editor, Frances Sevilla.
For my husband, Dave
who frees up my time; by doing chores and "horsework" he enables me to write.
For Laura Kelly who polished the first two books and helped them see the light of day.
And remembering the late Sharon Donovan, a talented writer who faced daunting health issues with such courage, and who would have been as thrilled as I am about this latest release in the "*Destiny*" series.

Chapter One

"Hold tight, Shifter, this is going to be bumpy."
The small vehicle careered down the incline, ploughing
a deep trough and throwing up a cloud of dirt and sand.
Eventually it plunged through the tangled branches of a
group of slender trees and bushes at the bottom, and
shuddered to a halt. For a moment, sandy soil and a blur
of green and brown severed leaves and twigs on the
external scanner obscured the view. Cat Kincaid ground
her teeth and activated a control.

A gust of recycled air blew away the offending
sand and foliage, and the screen before her displayed
the surrounding terrain. A bleak, undulating landscape,
punctuated by clumps of scrubby trees and bushes, like
the ones she'd crashed into, stretched into the distance.
A small forest bordered most of the far side of a steep
slope behind her. She grabbed her emergency pack, and
slung it over her shoulder, before swiping the airlock
control. *Let's hope the computer was right about the
atmosphere and pressure on this planet being
compatible with human requirements.*

"Come on Shifter," she called, and a large animal
materialized like a wraith from the shadows inside the
vehicle.

Two minutes later, after confirming the
temperature, pressure and air composition, Cat emerged
from her crippled craft. She gave a cautious sniff to the

1

air, then took a deeper breath, glancing up at a sullen, pale copper coloured sky. Although the atmosphere smelled a little sulphurous, the air was perfectly breathable. She stepped to the surface, and gave an involuntary start as the silence rent asunder with the unmistakable whine and shriek of blaster fire. She drew her pistol and ducked, using the hull of the craft as cover, acting on instinct, before logic cut in. Whoever it was, they weren't firing at her, and they were some distance away.

At least she wasn't alone. If life on this planet had advanced to a point where the inhabitants possessed power weapons, they might also have space vehicles, and be her means of escape—if she could just keep them from killing her.

She listened for a moment to confirm the direction of the firing. It came from somewhere beyond the rim of the sandy cliff behind her. It took several minutes to scramble to the top of the slope and peer cautiously above the edge.

The battle sounded closer now, coming from the other side of several low dunes looming before her. She bent low against a scorching wind that lashed the sand around her into swirling eddies. She cursed as it snatched several long strands of her hair from the scarf that struggled to restrain it at the nape of her neck. Like a dark red mist, the unbound hair whipped across her face, blurring her vision. She brushed it back, with a few more muttered words of annoyance. As she reached the top of another low hillock, the sky lit up with a scintillating green light and the sound of the weapons almost deafened her. Her fingers tightened on her laser pistol, and throwing herself to the ground, she inched her way to a group of thorny bushes for cover.

She strained to see how many combatants were involved. The air shimmered and danced in coruscating hues of blue and green, heavy with blaster smoke. Putting her tri-dee-viewer to her eyes, she adjusted the range. Three figures crouched behind a rock to one side of her in the shallow valley below. As far as she could make out, they were human. On the other side of the little clearing where the vegetation took over again, a much larger group, apparently also humanoid, kept up a relentless barrage of blaster fire. From this viewpoint, it looked as if they outnumbered the three several times over.

She raised her weapon undecided as to whether she should get involved or not. This was not her fight, especially since she didn't even know who they were. She drew in her breath. It would be cowardly just to leave. No one could call Cat Kincaid a coward, but she wasn't a fool either, nor about to commit suicide. However, allying herself with them might be her best hope of escape from this planet. A slight movement in the bushes just below her, to her right, and a low humming noise, warned her of another weapon firing up. A flash of light cut the air, and the shortest of the three figures gave a strangled cry, crumpling to the ground.

One of the men swung round and fired in their assailants' direction, while the other bent to tend to their companion.

Casting a quick look to her left, she took advantage of the confusion to check her surroundings. No sign of Shifter. She hoped he'd just merged into the landscape, but she couldn't risk checking, and could only trust he would find cover. The injury, or perhaps death, of one of the combatants lengthened the odds against them even further, making the decision for her. She couldn't just walk away from the situation.

One of the antagonists fired again, raising his head above the rock as he took aim. Cat fired back, rewarded by a shrill cry as the figure fell.

The metallic reek of blaster fire hung in the air, and the roar and whine of the weapons intensified. She flattened herself closer to the ground as another blaster bolt exploded into the dirt some distance from where she lay, scorching the sandy soil and shrivelling the undergrowth, sending down a cascade of small rocks and pebbles.

She rolled to the side as far as she could, at the same time, letting loose a few more bolts from her pistol. After several seconds, she risked a peek below her. One of the three, a dark haired man dressed in black, seemed to be holding his own and covering his two companions. A second man, blond haired and of slender build, knelt beside the motionless form of their fallen comrade. She made an adjustment to her weapon and flicked a control. At this rate, they could go on taking pot shots at the unknown enemy until they all died of starvation. She could at least shorten the odds a little.

Another crack of blaster fire caused her to duck for cover again. The salvo lasted for what seemed an interminable time. When the firing ceased, she risked another look. There was no sign of the other man or his wounded companion. The man in black crouched behind a rock.

*Where's the other one? Did he leave his friend to*

*fend off the attackers by himself?* She could not make him out clearly because of the distance, but he appeared to be alone.

*What happened to the one who'd been shot?*

She took the tri-dee-viewer from around her neck and focused it on the figure fighting a lone battle against an unknown number of opponents. He must be either very brave or very foolhardy. She adjusted the range and sucked in her breath. Even with his back toward her, something about his general physique and the way he held himself struck her as being almost familiar.

*Idiot. You're letting your imagination play tricks. You have no idea who that is down there, so why are you getting involved in the first place?*

Her priority must be to find a way off this planet. For now, though, she needed to get back to the safety of her escape vehicle before dark, but the likelihood of doing that seemed slimmer every moment. She pressed the trigger control and fired again.

\*\*\*\*

*Where did that damned smoke come from?* Kerry Marchant wiped his streaming eyes and tried to focus on the area where he last saw his attackers.

*Who are these people?* They had appeared from nowhere and fired at him and his two crewmates without warning or provocation. There was another question—the identity of the third party who seemed to be siding with them against their attackers. He turned back to glance at Jon Quinlan. The main concern, at the moment, was Zeldra.

"How is she?" he asked, indicating the unconscious woman.

The other man looked up from his ministrations, coughing and trying to waft some of the choking smoke away with his hand. "Not good. I've used my bio-regenerator and it's repaired some of the damage. We need to get her back to the *Destiny*."

"Then take her. At least this smoke will give you some cover. I'll hold them off here for as long as I can."

"What? And leave you here to fight them alone?"

"I can handle it. Come back for me."

"I don't like the thought of leaving you down here—"

"Have you a better idea? We can't both go. We would just be sitting targets if this smoke clears. I can cover you, but as the *Destiny's* commander, you need to be with the ship."

"We don't have time to argue—just make sure you stay in contact." The commander slung the woman's unconscious form over his shoulder and bending low beneath the smoke, edged his way back the way they'd come, keeping close to the tree-line. Kerry kept their attackers busy with a volley of well-aimed blaster fire.

*How many of them are there?* He must be hopelessly outnumbered, but he might as well be killed here as on some other planet. If only he could keep them busy long enough for Jon to get Zeldra safely to the *Destiny's* ferry craft.

He ducked behind the boulder as another volley of blaster fire singed the surrounding undergrowth. He fired once more and heard a strangled scream as another of his assailants went down.

A long silence ensued.

*What are they waiting for?* It seemed unlikely they were all dead or injured. However, an injured man, like a wounded animal, could be more dangerous than an uninjured one. He checked his blaster. The charge still held but it would not be long before it ran down.

He allowed another couple of minutes to elapse before risking a look. The smoke still hung in the air, although it seemed to be clearing a little. Apart from several bodies, the landscape seemed deserted. With all the caution he could muster, finger on the trigger button, he crept from around the rock. He froze. Sensing movement in the boulders opposite, he dived back again. Just as he reached the shelter of the rock, the ground seemed to explode around him. A piercing pain shot through his shoulder and he knew no more.

****

Cat paused and listened. The blaster fire ceased several minutes ago. The silence lay thick and as heavy as the smoke after the din of power weapons moments before.

She should have been long gone. *I should leave now, while I still can.*

The effects of the smoke capsule she'd released would not last long. Already the air was becoming clearer. She turned once more and trained her viewer back on the clump of rocks. The man in black lay motionless.

*Leave him. Leave him and get out of here.* If she was right and he and his companions *were* human, presumably they'd have some sort of transit ship, unless their starship was small enough for planetary landings. Either way, they'd surely come back for him.

Then it dawned on her that if they returned, perhaps she could persuade—or force—them to take her with them. If he was alive, he'd serve as a bargaining chip.

She checked her weapon and looked down again on the scene of the recent battle. A gray haze still hung over the area, the motionless figure on the ground barely visible in the gloom. There were no other signs of life. She waited a few more minutes and let off another shot. No response. Either their assailants were dead, or they had escaped under the cover of smoke. Perhaps they believed they'd killed the three people they'd been firing on, although nagging caution warned her it seemed strange they did not come back to check. Holding her gun in both hands ready to fire, every nerve alert, she pushed the thought to one side and made her way down to where the fallen man lay.

A spreading crimson stain showed on his shoulder and chest. Shards of rock lay everywhere, most of it from the large boulder he'd sheltered behind, split down the middle almost in two pieces. It must have absorbed most of the blast so he missed the main force. It looked like the wound was caused by the shattering rock, or the damage would have been a whole lot worse, and she probably wouldn't have been able to do anything for him.

She knelt and drew in her breath.

*Kerry Marchant.* She'd only seen holograms of the man. She could not recall noticing the faint scar beneath his left eye before, but it must be him. He'd changed little in the five years since she first saw the images, after searching through countless holo-libraries, and those features were unforgettable. She allowed herself the hint of a smile. She'd always hoped one day she'd run into him, and now fate played right into her hands.

For a fleeting moment, she thought of killing him

there and then, but she was not a cold-blooded murderer. She could just leave him, let him bleed to death, but she wanted to be the instrument of his demise when it came. She wanted him to know who killed him—and why. Besides, she had questions only he could answer.

His gun lay nearby and she grabbed it with one hand, without taking her eyes off him, and slipped it under her belt. His eyes were closed, his face pale but his breathing steady. She needed to work quickly before he regained consciousness. Not that she was sure she could help him anyway. It depended on the extent of the damage.

Glancing warily around before holstering her own gun, she slid her emergency pack from her shoulder. She rummaged inside and brought out a compressed blanket. Taking it from its container, she waited until it fluffed out, and folded it into a thick pad to support his head. Next, she took her medical kit and laid it on the ground while she attempted to unfasten his tunic. In the warm air, the blood dried quickly, and the leather-like material stuck to the wound. She would need to cut his shirt.

A silver chain hung around his neck with a small oblong metal capsule. Cat hesitated for a moment, before curiosity got the better of her, and she flipped open the lid. A soft, cushioning material lined the interior. She tipped the contents into her hand—a tiny gold cross and a locket. A quick glance at the inside of the locket revealed the portrait of a young woman with short dark hair curving in soft waves to frame her face, blue eyes, and a long, aquiline nose. The family resemblance looked too close for it to be a wife or girlfriend, so perhaps the image portrayed his sister or mother. Swiftly, she replaced the two items.

As Cat bent over him, her hair, now loosened completely from the scarf, swung forward, and she shook it back from her face with an impatient gesture. She took her knife from her belt, and inserted the point into the material of his tunic.

At once, a hand reached up and grabbed her wrist, with fingers like cold, carbon steel.

## Chapter Two

For a man who was unconscious only a few seconds before, he had a surprisingly firm grip.

His eyes flicked open. They were the most unusual shade of blue she'd ever seen, reminiscent of the cerulean tones of glacial strata and about as chilly. No holographic image could ever accurately convey that colour. They widened, and in their depths, Cat saw what she could only translate as complete shock and disbelief, coupled with what seemed like a flicker of recognition. But he couldn't have recognized her. They'd never met before. She'd only ever seen holograms of him, and there could be no reason why he should have seen images of her.

He stared at her for a second, before his expression changed to something that could almost have been despair. A deep-seated pain that she sensed bore no relation to his injury. A moment later, the lines of his face hardened, and his hold on her wrist became even firmer so she had to clench her teeth to stop herself from yelping.

"Drop the knife."

The voice was weak, but deep, with a distinctive timbre. At least he spoke *Common Universal*. She tried to wrench herself free.

"Let go of me before you break my wrist. Can't you see I'm trying to help you? Let me go," she repeated, when he showed no sign of relaxing his grasp. "I need to cut open your shirt to see how bad the wound is. If I meant any harm, don't you think you'd be dead by now?" He did not reply, and she went on, "Are you going to let me tend to your wound or not? I can just as easily leave you here to bleed to death, if you'd prefer."

The fingers eased their vice-like grip. "There's…a bio-regenerator…in my hip pocket…I need to get it."

"Slowly then, no sudden moves." She waved the knife to emphasize her meaning.

She stood back as he slowly withdrew the small instrument from his pocket. The effort seemed to drain him, and his face grew even paler. "Just press the lever…on the edge to activate it. Then…run it over the wound…take care not to touch…the under-surface."

"I could've probably worked that out for myself," she muttered, her voice laced with sarcasm, and felt a momentary twang of guilt at her impatience. He must be in pain. No need to get irritated because he tried to prevent her from injuring herself. In an instant, she dismissed the thought from her mind. Too bad. If she had her way, he'd suffer a lot more than a few sharp words once he'd told her what she needed to know.

Carefully slicing open the tunic, she checked the wound in his chest. Deep and jagged, it seemed to be only a flesh wound and probably nothing vital was damaged, although it still bled profusely. She ran the instrument over the injury, amazed to see the blood clot, and a rapid regrowth of new skin form over it. In a few seconds, it healed almost completely. His shoulder had also sustained severe lacerations in addition to the vivid purple bruises forming on the skin. She repeated the operation with the device. The bruises faded and the torn flesh knitted together barely leaving a scar.

She replaced the knife in her belt, and in a deft movement pulled her hair back and knotted the scarf around it once more. "Impressive. How d'you feel?"

"It seems I will survive," he said in the slow, precise tones that made his voice so distinctive. "Thank you," he added, almost as an afterthought. He reached for the bio-regenerator and stashed it back in his pocket. His face gained some colour, and a minute or two later, he was unrecognizable from the man she'd found wounded and bleeding a short while ago.

"What is that, anyway—what did you call it—*a bio-regenerator*?"

"Exactly. It does, as you see, precisely what you would expect, including destroying any toxins or bacteria present in the wound."

She inclined her head as she considered his words. "It's not Terran." She meant it as an observation rather than a question.

"The technology was given to us by a race called the Phidians."

"I've heard of them. Their advances in medicine are well known." She looked up at the heavens. "About time we got away from here. Night isn't too far off by the look of that sky." The light faded perceptibly while they spoke and the air took on a noticeable chill after the earlier oppressive heat.

"What about our 'friends'?" He turned his head and looked in the direction of the rocks where the assailants of a few minutes before let loose the last salvo of blaster fire.

She put the tri-dee-viewer to her eyes again and scanned the area. "There's no sign of life over there.

They must all be dead or badly injured. They'd have shot at us again if they were still capable."

"Unless they are waiting for us to show ourselves, so they can pick us off more easily," Kerry said.

He made as if to stand, and in an instant, she drew her pistol.

"Like I said before, no sudden moves. Get up—slowly."

"So you are making me a prisoner?"

"Not exactly, but I'm not stupid enough to take any risks."

He rose to his feet, his gaze not leaving her gun-hand. Several inches taller than her, broad shouldered and slim, he presented a commanding figure. His expression froze as his gaze homed in on the insignia on her breast pocket, his eyes like chips of blue ice. "You work for the Union."

"I work for myself."

"Then why are you wearing the insignia of the Global Union of Earth and Allied Planets?"

"I have a license to requisition any enemy ship trespassing in the sectors of space over which they hold dominion."

"A licensed pirate in the pay of the Global Union," Kerry's eyes showed outright contempt. She almost preferred the icy coolness.

"I prefer to think of myself as a freelancer—doing a service."

His expression did not change, although he did change tack. "You could have left me to die—or just shot me. Why didn't you?"

"Call it a personality flaw. I don't like abandoning someone who's wounded even to save my own skin.

And I don't kill in cold blood. If I have to shoot someone, I'd rather they were facing me with their eyes open." *Even if I did swear to leave their dead body for the Union to use in their hideous experiments. Keep it casual. Don't let him guess what's really in your mind.*

To her amazement, he smiled the most devastating smile she'd ever seen, made even more remarkable because he didn't look as if he did it very often.

"My own philosophy as it happens. It seems almost a pity we are on opposite sides."

"Opposite sides?"

"I have no love for the Union. That puts us on opposite sides, even if you are just a pirate, doing their dirty work for them."

She gave him her best withering look. "Fine. And just because I decided to save your hide, don't get any ideas. We don't have to like each other."

"I was merely alluding to the fact we seem to have a similar moral code."

"I doubt it." She waved her weapon in the direction of the rocks, where the firing had come from earlier, while bending to retrieve her supply pack and thermal blanket, still keeping her gaze fixed on him. "We need to make sure whoever was shooting at you and your friends is really dead. Move, and remember I'm not letting you out of my sight."

They reached the rock their adversaries had used as a shield. With her finger on the trigger button Cat swung round it, prepared to fire if anyone moved. Then she froze. The area was clear. Not the bodies she expected to find, no sign anyone had ever been there at all.

She looked at Kerry. "They were here. They can't

have just vanished."

He shook his head. "Unless they can teleport—which has been proven to be impossible by mechanical means. It is just possible they may have psionic capabilities."

"No point in worrying about them now. Seems they've gone, however they did it." Cat gave a long low whistle and one of the nearby boulders morphed into the tawny form of Shifter.

"What the hell is that?" As if acting on instinct, Kerry reached for his gun and then swore softly when his fingers failed to close upon it. His gaze flicked toward her. He cursed again and stared pointedly at his blaster thrust through her belt.

She ignored his stare and nodded toward the animal. "His name's Shifter. He's…well, I call him a chameleopard, and I'd kill anyone who tried to shoot him."

Kerry favoured her with a cold look. "Delightful pets you have."

"It's only one, and yes, he is quite cute actually. Are you going to be able to walk?"

"It was my chest that was injured, not my legs."

She ignored his sarcastic tone. Gratitude obviously did not feature among his finer points.

"My vehicle's not far away, about half a klick." She paused. "What were you doing down here anyway? This planet isn't even listed on the charts. I wouldn't be here myself out of choice."

"We were looking for you," Kerry said in his slow, laconic manner. "Our ship picked up the distress signal your escape vessel transmitted as it hit the atmosphere. Had we chosen to ignore it, we would have been in violation of the Universal Code." A small crease furrowed his brow. "We set our ferry down close to where our computer predicted you would crash-land. As soon as we stepped foot on the planet we were fired upon with no warning, although our on-board sensors indicated there were no life forms in the immediate vicinity."

Cat nodded. "Some welcoming committee." She struck up a brisk pace, making sure she kept him ahead of her and within her range of vision. The irony of the situation was not lost on her. He'd come to rescue her, and she ended up coming to his aid instead—the last person she wanted to give assistance to or accept help from.

She gave him a sideways glance. He appeared to have recovered from his injury in a remarkably short space of time due, no doubt, to the miraculous properties of the instrument he called a bio-regenerator. Now that would be worth a small fortune in the right hands. The Union would undoubtedly be very interested in this man and his ship. What other inventions did the *Destiny's* crew have that might be of interest to them?

Her musings were cut short as they surmounted the final hillock and edged sideways down the incline to the shallow basin where her vessel lay, almost hidden, beneath the low hanging branches of the bushes into which it had crashed. She glanced up. The first stars twinkled above the three moons in the darkening sky. At least they'd made it before nightfall.

"You landed that well," he said, scrutinizing the vehicle.

"Not particularly. I crash-landed."

"I was being facetious."

"She took a battering in an electric storm as we came in. It only lasted a few minutes, but it was bad enough to wreck the flight controls." *Why do I need to explain anything to him anyway?* "At least the bushes give some cover. I'll put a force-shield up overnight. I just didn't want to drain her power packs after I crashed." She touched a panel on the ship's hull, and after a moment, a hatch slid open with a slight hiss. Shifter leapt in immediately but Kerry stood back as she climbed into the airlock.

She turned with her gun still trained on him. "Are you coming? Or would you prefer to take your chances out there all night?"

He shrugged and followed her inside. They waited in the eerie blue light until the inner door opened.

She walked across to the control panel at the front of the cabin and made a few adjustments. A gentle glow illuminated the interior. "It's not much, but it's likely to be home for a while until I can find a way off this planet. There wouldn't be enough left in the fuel cells now to get far in this, even if I could repair the damage."

He looked around, his face expressionless.

She frowned at his perusal. The furnishings of the small interior were necessarily sparse. A pilot seat and passenger seat to the front, and at the rear of the vessel, a small living and storage area, complete with a folding table and murphy bunk unit. If he didn't like it, too bad. He could always go back outside and sleep rough if he preferred.

"I dare say it will suffice," he said at length.

"Well, thank you. I'm so glad it meets with your approval."

His expression remained impassive. It seemed her cynicism was lost on him. "It would be useful to have a name to call you."

"Catrina. Catrina…Kincaid. I prefer to be called Cat."

Again, that stunning smile spread over his face, and she noticed how his eyes seemed even bluer above the even, white teeth. Damn, there was something about him. She almost regretted she'd have to kill him eventually.

"The name suits you." It did not sound like a compliment. "I am Kerry Marchant."

"Yes, I know who you are." She ignored his quizzical look. "As I said earlier, don't get any ideas. This 'cat' has claws."

"I don't doubt it."

She activated the small cleansing unit housed in an alcove set into the bulkhead and ran her hands through the antiseptic mist. "How's the shoulder? D'you want me to look at it?"

"No need. The regenerator seems to have done its job." He unclipped his pack and withdrew a compressed black garment. "Is there somewhere I can clean up and change my tunic?"

"Help yourself. There's a washroom back there," she said, indicating a small door behind him. While he was occupied, she went to the storage unit and removed a metal container. Taking another vessel, she poured water from it into the first, and tipped the resulting reconstituted raw meat on a large plate she placed on the floor. Shifter stuck his nose in it and gulped it down in several mouthfuls, without pausing for breath, before drinking from the bowl of water she placed before him.

After a few minutes, Kerry reappeared, having replaced his ruined shirt. He regarded the chameleopard with an expression of curiosity on his face.

"Interesting animal. Where did you get him?"

"I found him on a small planet in the Andromeda system. He'd been bred for fighting. I don't agree with keeping animals to kill each other, so I fought his owner for him. Fed properly and treated well he's actually quite docile—unless he feels he has to protect me."

Those cold eyes betrayed nothing, but he looked at her as if not sure whether to believe her.

"I suppose you're hungry too. It's only normal ship's survival rations, but they'll keep us going for a while."

"Then that will have to do."

*Of all the ungrateful...* She turned to the dispenser unit and, for a split second, dropped her guard. In the same instant, she felt an arm whip around her throat.

## Chapter Three

Cat froze, trying to catch her breath, and clenching her fists in frustration. *Damn, how could I have been so careless?*

Kerry removed both her gun and his own from her belt, together with her knife, before releasing his stranglehold.

"Did you really think I would stand by and let you take my gun without trying to get it back?" He gave her a none-too-gentle shove between the shoulder blades, with what felt like the muzzle of one of the guns. "Don't let me stop you from carrying on with what you were doing."

"Go to hell. Shoot me in the back if you must. I'll be damned if I'll be your slave." As she spoke, she kicked back with all her force. Her heel connected with his shin, knocking him off balance. Whirling round, she made use of her momentary advantage to snatch back her gun and level it at his chest. "Try that again and I'll blow your head off. Now give me back your firearm."

His eyes glimmered and the blue ice turned to steel. "When *hell* freezes over. Do you think I'm just going to hand over my blaster and let you shoot me when I'm not looking?"

"We've had this conversation before. If I'd wanted to shoot you, I'd have done it straight away and saved myself the trouble of getting you back here." She gave him a jab in the ribs with the barrel of her pistol by way of emphasis.

"Then why are you still pointing a gun at me?"

For a long moment, he held her with his gaze. She felt her skin tingle, and quivers of awareness chased themselves up and down her spine. Without speaking, and watching him like a predator watches its prey, she lowered her weapon as he laid his on the table between them.

"And my knife."

His face expressionless, he laid the knife on the table beside the gun.

After a moment, she picked up his gun and placed it into another compartment in the bulkhead, together with both her own weapons. "I don't want you strangling me in the night because you're afraid I might shoot you or stab you in your sleep. Don't get any ideas either, I can look after myself, armed or not."

"I hope for your sake nothing, or no-one, attacks us in the night."

"Don't worry, I'll protect you," she said, mimicking his mocking tone. "And I told you, the vessel will be shielded, and any intruders are going to be sorry if they try to break through. As for the gun, you can have it back as soon as I know I can trust you."

*Unless your friends come back for you, in which case you'll be my ticket off this planet.*

His face betrayed no emotion. *Curse him.* What was going on behind those amazing, if ice-cold, eyes?

She laid the food before him and they ate in silence. Survival rations were not the tastiest of meals but at least they were filling. The meal over, he again gave her that inscrutable look which for some reason she found so disturbing

"I need to ask another favour."

"*Really*?" She inclined her head to one side and tried to conceal her curiosity with a hint of scorn in her voice.

"Yes. I need to use your sub-space radio to contact my ship. I'm anxious to know if the other two reached it safely. Zeldra was quite badly injured." He raked his hand through his hair in a gesture she interpreted as meaning he was more concerned than he wanted to admit. "My communicator must have been damaged during the fight out there. I should have heard from the ship by now."

"You can try the unit in here, assuming it's still operational. We had a pretty rough landing, as I said." She paused. "But there's a condition."

His eyes glinted, his mouth set in a hard line. Perhaps she'd over-stepped the mark. She could hold her own with most men, but this one was a little bit different—a little bit dangerous. Meeting his cool stare, she said calmly, "I want you to take me with you when your ship's crew comes back for you."

He raised an eyebrow. "You expect me to promise that…after you just threatened to kill me?"

"I also saved your life. How else will I get off this planet? Anyway, you did say you came to rescue me." She glared at him. "If you don't agree, just forget about using my radio…or getting your gun back."

"I would not have taken you for a blackmailer."

"It's not blackmail, just survival, and you haven't known me long enough to 'take me' for anything."

"I can well believe it," he said, with what could almost have been a touch of humour in that

23

disconcerting rich, dark voice. "All right, since you are so persuasive, I agree to your terms."

He followed her to the control panel and seated himself before it.

"You know how to operate it? It's not standard issue."

"I think I can manage."

The way his fingers flew over the panel, connecting with the various controls, convinced her he could more than manage. The instrument's lights flickered and the panel glowed into life. After several attempts and a lot of static, he sighed in exasperation. "The radio is working all right, but the signal's not getting through. It must be solar flare activity." His eyes narrowed and a twitch played at the corner of his mouth. "I'm a little worried. We have two Nifl telepaths on board. I would have expected one of them to have contacted me by now."

"Can't you contact *them*?"

He looked slightly annoyed as if she were asking him to explain the obvious.

"*I* am not a telepath. Telepaths can project their thoughts to non-telepaths, it doesn't work the other way round."

Having consigned the reusable utensils to the sanitization unit, she touched a control and the table folded away, replaced by two bunks designed for convenience more than comfort.

"I'll take the top one, you can have the bottom. Remember, I'm a light sleeper and so's Shifter."

Kerry did not give the appearance of being a man inclined to submit to warnings, but the words made her feel she was in charge of the situation.

She needed to be in control. Yet she could not deny, even to herself, he both excited and disturbed her, and she could not remember ever having felt that way before. Too bad she'd sworn to kill him.

****

This was not working out as planned. They had assumed it would be a quick trip to the surface in response to a distress call and then a direct return to the *Destiny*. Instead, Kerry found himself separated from the crew and sharing a meal with a woman who appeared to be working for the Union. If not quite sharing her bed, at least her hospitality, even if she did give that hospitality somewhat grudgingly.

The loss of communication with the *Destiny* concerned him. He needed to contact Jon to be sure the commander and Zeldra had made it back to the *Destiny*. The atmospheric analyses he ran before they landed gave no indication the signals would not be able to pass through the planet's atmosphere, so the worrying lack of contact must be attributable to unusual solar flare activity. He could think of no other logical explanation.

His attention turned to Cat. The woman was an enigma. Although she seemed not to care too much for human life, she stayed to tend him when he lay injured. She could have left him to die and no one would have been any the wiser.

The long red hair, freed again from its restraining scarf, fell around her shoulders, giving her a softer, more feminine look than when she'd worn it tied back. Not that the way the basic tight fitting space tunic and slacks clung to her curves left any doubt about her gender.

That hair! Just for a fleeting moment, when he first

saw her through a haze of pain and confusion, he imagined…he shook his head to dispel the vision flooding his memory. The grief, the almost physical ache he endeavoured to hide, still remained; a constant reminder of what might have been.

He studied her face again: high cheekbones and a finely chiselled face, flawless skin and full lips. The eyes, a clear gray, at times looked almost silver. She was certainly attractive enough, although not the striking beauty Jess had been. Something else about her, apart from the hair, seemed disturbingly familiar, although he could not remember who she reminded him of.

"Is there a problem?"

He brought himself back to reality with an effort. "What makes you ask?"

"You were looking at me as if…as if you were seeing someone else."

He looked at her through narrowed eyes without dropping his gaze. She was too perceptive for his liking. "I was just wondering what you're doing here, and what happened to your ship."

"Not that it's any of your business," she said, a cold edge to her voice, "but my ship was hi-jacked. I managed to get away in the only escape vessel."

"Then you were willing to leave your crew to their fate in order to save your own neck?" He did not attempt to keep the contempt out of his voice. "Yet, you took the time to fix me up and bring me back here. It seems a little inconsistent."

She smiled, her lips parting in a way he found almost sensuous. "I'm not completely devoid of feelings. I'd have done the same for any wounded creature—animal or human." She paused for several seconds. "As for leaving my crew to their fate, yes, it was a sacrifice, but since they were androids—"

"Androids?" Then she was not just a callous adventuress willing to sacrifice others to save her own skin, after all. Not that it made any difference. She worked for the Union and, by her own admission, stole ships for them. "I have never heard of a pirate ship with an android crew. Piracy must pay well these days."

"I never said I was a pirate. That was *your* assumption."

"No? Then what exactly do you say you are?"

Again, a hint of a smile spread across her face, and she paused before replying. "As I told you before, I prefer the term 'freelancer,' or 'privateer,' if you insist."

"You steal ships for the Global Union. That's just another form of piracy as far as I'm concerned."

She shrugged, as if to indicate it was of little consequence to her what he thought.

"I don't hold with the way the Global Union operates," he went on. "I have done a few things myself that I'm not exactly proud of, but even in my book, piracy is a crime."

She threw back her head and laughed, not quite the reaction he'd expected. Her face softened when she laughed, lightening the contours of her face. The difference it made was remarkable. Under different circumstances…

He forced himself to concentrate on the present as she met his gaze.

"I get the feeling perhaps you're not one of the Union's greatest advocates," she said, still with a slight upturning of her lips.

"You could say that. What were you doing 'privateering' for the Union in this quadrant anyway? According to our ship's computer, there are no other ships and no warring factions in this sector of space, so if you *are* a privateer, you wouldn't have any reason to be in this region of space at all, the pickings would be pretty lean. Suppose you tell me the truth? What is going on?"

"You're asking me that? I was hoping you could tell me. As I said before, this nondescript corner of the galaxy wasn't exactly high on my list of places to visit."

He sighed in exasperation, ignoring the glint of humour in her eyes. He was not in the mood to play games and this woman did nothing to allay his natural mistrust of women in general. He was almost positive she was lying to him. What was she trying to hide? Tomorrow could not come quick enough. Tomorrow, with any luck, the solar flares should have abated so he could contact the *Destiny* and return to the ship. Then they could decide what to do with this "pirate queen," or whatever she was, and find out what she was really up to.

\*\*\*\*

Kerry spent several hours trying to diagnose the fault on his communicator. He found nothing to account for its failure, and by all the laws of physics, the instrument should have worked perfectly, but stubbornly remained silent, even after he replaced the master chip. He was also getting some very strange readings, which he could only assume were also due to solar flares. Eventually he decided to admit defeat and succumb to a few hours' sleep.

His dreams were full of visions of a young woman with long red hair that shone like fire in the starlight, and whose emerald green eyes kept changing unaccountably to silver-gray.

As soon as his chrono alerted him to the time, a few minutes before dawn, he slid over the side of the bunk. He'd slept fully dressed, apart from his boots, which he pulled on with some haste before walking over to where Cat stood by the small replicating unit.

"Coffee?"

He took the proffered container and sipped, enjoying the warmth. "I'm going to try to contact the *Destiny* again, *if* that is all right by you?"

She ignored the slight sarcasm of the emphasis placed on the word "if." "Sure. Go ahead. I've lifted the shield so it won't block the signal."

He drained the cup and set it down before making his way to the communications control panel. After several minutes, he scowled in exasperation.

"It seems we are stuck here until I can make contact with my ship, or until she can contact me on my personal communicator…except that still doesn't seem to be working either. I took it to pieces last night and checked each component thoroughly. There is no technical reason why it should not both receive and transmit. The only logical explanation is abnormal solar energy activity but there is no way to confirm it."

"So what do you intend to do?"

"I need to go back to the area where we left the *Destiny*'s ferry," he said. "At least if it is no longer there, I will know Jon got Zeldra back to the ship safely."

Cat settled herself beside him at the controls. "I'll scan the area again, to make sure it's safe to go outside. I ran a preliminary scan earlier while you were still asleep. There don't appear to be any other life forms around, at least not in the immediate vicinity."

He was already aware she'd run some sort of scan. At least, he assumed that was what she did, as he watched her through half-closed eyes, when she thought he was asleep.

She tapped out a few commands on the control panel. "I really miss not having a sentient computer." After a few moments, the shield slid back from the forward observation panel. No movement disturbed the branches of their cover, no sign of life, not even small animals, or birds.

"What about the peripheral area?" he asked.

Cat touched another control and the transmitters from the external scanners relayed a panoramic view of the surrounding countryside. The reddish brown hillocks and dunes above the rim, partially shrouded in early morning mist, merged into a haze of grayish green where they joined the tree line, but there were no unusual features, and nothing to disturb the tranquillity of the landscape. Cat made another sweep, just to make sure. The instruments registered no obvious sign of life or movement.

He tried the communicator on his wrist again. "Jon, Delian, Berne…is there anyone on the *Destiny* who can hear me?"

When there was again no response, he glanced at Cat and shook his head in frustration.

"If it's not solar flare activity, either something has happened to the *Destiny*, or they have moved from stationary orbit and are out of range of my transceiver. If that were the case, I should have been able to reach them via the radio." He ran an impatient hand through his hair. "I can't believe Jon would not have tried to contact me if they had to do that, but the device is registering no incoming messages. Even if he could not get through immediately, there should at least be a trace to indicate he tried."

"Well, there's not much point staying here, and Shifter needs to go outside. Coming?"

He had almost forgotten the animal, until a part of the flooring moved and revealed itself as the chameleopard. The way its coat changed to mimic the colour of whatever object it stood close to intrigued him. The trait was similar to that of the Terran reptile it had presumably been named after by Cat. It blended so well with its surroundings that, until it moved, it remained almost invisible. To him, the creature resembled a large Terran wolf, although its long, sharp fangs were more like tusks than teeth. Shifter seemed tractable enough around Cat, but he would not like to be on the receiving end of a bite from those teeth.

He checked his emergency pack. "Do I get my blaster? I don't fancy going out there unarmed."

She hesitated for a moment then removed the heavy weapon from the compartment where she'd placed it the previous evening. She handed it to him wordlessly, keeping hold of her own gun, her finger hovering just above the trigger control. She followed his gaze as he glanced down at her weapon, and answered his questioning look with one of her own.

"That is an unusual looking weapon you have there," he stated.

"I designed it myself," she said, and he caught a hint of pride in her voice. "It's a combination of a laser and a blaster. It can also be modified to use as a tool if necessary and has a few other enhancements. So don't get any ideas," she added, "I'm fully capable of using it."

"I don't doubt it," he said, with grudging admiration. "Your own design, you said?"

"It was one of my occupations in another lifetime. Are we going to stand around here all day or see if we can find some way off this planet?" She pulled out a couple of objects from the same recess in the bulkhead. "Better have one of these too."

He eyed the communicator she passed him. "Do I need this?"

"If we're going to be out there facing an unknown enemy, we need to be able to keep in touch in case we get separated. I assume your own communicator will be on a totally different frequency to mine, and you'll need to maintain the current settings in case your ship manages to contact you."

She had a point. He nodded and slipped it on his left wrist, above his own communicator and scanner. They descended to the planet's surface once more.

Cat activated a small control on her pistol. At once, the air around the vehicle shimmered and sparkled. She bent down and threw a small pebble at the escape craft. The pebble glowed, and with a bright flash, crumbled to dust. "Good, the shield is still working. I was afraid there might not be enough power left, it was pretty well drained yesterday, but it should soon charge up in the daylight."

Cat whistled to the chameleopard, and they

climbed the slope and walked in silence for some time, retracing their steps of the previous day. The atmosphere, heavy and oppressive, made talking a luxury when even breathing became an effort, and kept their pace necessarily slow. Even the ceaseless wind felt warm and provided no respite from the heat. When they reached the scene of the previous day's battle, they once more searched the area. There was no sign that anything had ever happened there. The rock behind which he sheltered the previous day stood, rent in two, but there were no signs of bodies, and the ground showed no evidence of any disturbance.

Several more minutes walking brought them to where the *Destiny's* ferry set down the previous day. He glanced at Cat and she nodded. They drew their weapons. The area gave the appearance of being deserted, but after the anomalies of the day before, it would be foolish to make assumptions or take unnecessary risks.

When he activated the device attached to his belt and it showed no indication they were in the vicinity of a cloaked object, he breathed a sigh of relief. At least he knew the craft had been able to take off, and it was reasonably safe to assume they'd made it to the *Destiny*.

"There's nothing here," Cat observed, after checking her own instrument.

"That's right. There is nothing here…now. With any luck, that means they got back to the *Destiny* and once they can get in contact, we will be able to ask them to send down a vehicle for us."

"Won't be too soon for me."

He could not shake off the sense of foreboding that grew stronger the more time passed with no word from the *Destiny*. "I would give a lot to know what is preventing us from contacting each other. If the *Destiny* had been attacked by another ship—" He broke off and gave her a searching look.

"Don't look at me, I work alone."

"Well, if there was a space battle, we would have known about it. Apart from the fact your own instruments should have registered such an event, the *Destiny* is in close stationary orbit. We would have seen the pyrotechnics."

"So what do you suggest?"

"There is no point just hanging around here. We should go back to your escape vehicle. At least we have shelter there." He turned and headed back in the direction of the craft. "How badly is it damaged?" he asked over his shoulder. "Are you sure it's not repairable?"

"Doubtful. The propulsion and nav-units are probably done for," she said, catching up with him, "not to mention the fuel cells."

"Then we're stuck here until I can make contact with the ship." Her computer's data banks indicated there was intelligent life on this planet, but not that it was particularly advanced. He stopped at the top of one of the sandy hillocks that seemed to be a feature of this particular area, and looked across at the area where Cat had found him yesterday. Bodies could not vanish without trace. There had to be some explanation. "Judging by the reception we received yesterday, it seems they shoot first rather than asking questions. We are not likely to get any help from that quarter, even if we find an inhabited settlement."

"You think they were natives of this planet, then?"

"They didn't introduce themselves," he said, with a slight lift of his shoulders. "However, it is too much of a coincidence for another ship to have landed at the same time we did and decided to shoot at us without challenging us or revealing their identity. As far as our computer's sweeps and scans could determine, there is nothing of particular interest here. No mineral or crystal deposits of any value to opportunists." He pushed his hair back with his hand and drew his brows together in a frown. "Besides, there would have been an energy signature or some evidence of another ship in orbit around the planet. Unless of course it went back into hyper-space before the *Destiny* arrived."

"And whoever it was who attacked you, they seem to have vanished without a trace," Cat said, biting her bottom lip while she considered. "There were no bodies left behind, and yet some of them were definitely hit. I know I got several myself. How did they get away with their wounded so quickly?"

Kerry shook his head. "If I knew the answer to that I would be—"

Before he could continue, Cat stopped abruptly. "Hold it a moment. Look, over there."

Chapter Four

Kerry followed the direction of Cat's gaze.

"I hadn't noticed before, but there seems to be a building in the middle of nowhere. Strange how I've only just seen it, and why should there be any structures out here with no other sign of habitation or civilization at all?"

He focused his tri-dee viewer on the large structure in the distance, half hidden among some trees to the northwest. "I'm not sure. I've not seen it before either." He checked the small instrument attached to his wrist, above the communicator bands. "More importantly, there appears to be some sort of signal emanating from it."

"Well I'm not keen to investigate. We've already established that the natives aren't particularly friendly."

He checked the pulsing of the signal. The pattern was consistent with the universal code for a request for assistance. He narrowed his eyes as he looked at her. "It could be a trap, or it might be a genuine distress signal. We can hardly ignore it."

"Then let's go, instead of just talking about it. But I have to tell you, I have a bad feeling about that place…and my hunches are usually right."

As it happened, he shared Cat's concerns, but it had to be checked out. He was still not sure he felt ready to give her his complete trust. She had helped him when he was injured, but he harboured no doubt that if he made a move she perceived as threatening, she would not hesitate to shoot him. She must have similar misgivings about him, of course. Good. While each was watching the other, they would stay alert to any dangers. The available data on the planet was sparse. This sector of space was, according to all the computer data, unexplored. Therefore, they had to rely mainly on what little information the *Destiny's* computer and scanners had been able to extrapolate. There could be any number of threats lurking out there.

The building, when they eventually reached it, gave the impression of being unoccupied and derelict. Built of large reddish stone slabs, the structure was comprised of three stories. The architecture was peculiar, almost like an ancient Mayan pyramid of old Earth, but with small windows completely covered with a layer of dirt, making it impossible to see into the interior. A blood red, lichen-like plant covered the walls, vying for space with another creeping plant of a similar khaki colour to much of the other vegetation in the area. An imposing and very solid looking wooden panelled door guarded the entrance.

He checked the instrument on his wrist once more. "The signal is definitely coming from inside the building. It is very strong now." He drew his blaster and glanced behind him to where Cat stood near his shoulder, her own handgun ready for action.

To his surprise, when he put his hand on the large, metal handle, and turned it, the door gave slightly, but then appeared to be jammed. He did not intend to risk his injured chest and shoulder, even though to all intents and purposes it was now fully healed. "Stand back," he hissed and his laser made short work of the hinges. A push with his thick-soled boot sent the door crashing inward.

"Well if there's anyone inside, they know we're here now," Cat remarked with dry humour.

"There isn't," he said, checking his hand scanner and ignoring her sarcasm. There were more serious things to worry about. "There are no life-signs registering on my bio-scanner."

"I don't like it," she said. "My instincts aren't often wrong."

"Suit yourself, but I want to get to the bottom of that signal. It's getting stronger and the sequence is definitely a distress code."

"You have a wrist flare?"

"Of course."

"Come on then, if we're going in." Cat turned to look over her shoulder. "Shifter, stay here. Don't wander too far."

"He understands what you say?" Two could play at sarcastic.

She glared at him. "Not word for word, but he understands enough."

They stepped across the ruined door and into the building, scanning the giant shadows cast by their wrist flares for any movement caused by something other than themselves. Inside the building, the air hung damp and chill, although the temperature outside remained hot and sultry.

He glanced around the walls and cast the light from his flare into the corners. Anything could be lurking in the gloom. He did not say as much to Cat, but despite his assurances and the absence of life signs on the instrumentation he did not feel fully convinced the building was as deserted as it appeared. He intended to take no chances. Someone must have set up the distress signal. They just might have walked into a trap, and despite being undetected by his scanner, someone or something could be hiding in the darkness awaiting their chance.

On the ground floor they found three small rooms and another, much larger, with a winding staircase at one end. Nothing alleviated the stark bareness of the rooms. A thick layer of dust covered everything. Anyone recently in the building would have left noticeable footprints.

Every nerve tensed, he frowned at the woman beside him. Something was not right. Why should there be a distress signal coming from this isolated, deserted building far from where his instrumentation told him the nearest settlement might be?

He checked his scanner again as Cat moved a little way ahead of him. The signal seemed to come from somewhere above them. While Cat made a cautious ascent of the stairs, her pistol at the ready, he swept his flare toward the low ceiling, searching every cranny where a device might be hidden.

Engrossed though he was in his search, his actions were instantaneous the moment the signal stopped.

He leapt across the floor toward the staircase. "Get out now, it's a trap!"

As Cat half turned, he grabbed hold of her arm and dragged her from the stairs toward the doorway, throwing himself down and pulling her with him. A deep rumble became a deafening roar, as stones and rubble rained down on them, burying them beneath the choking dust.

****

Kerry opened his eyes and wondered how he could still breathe. He blinked to clear the dust from his eyes. He remembered with crystal clarity the last few seconds before the explosion. The device must have been very small or the building would have collapsed completely and buried them alive. In fact, most of the rubble he lay beneath appeared to be dust and debris thrown up by the explosion. The walls themselves were still standing.

*What an idiot.* He'd walked straight into it. He must be losing his mind. Instinct told him it was a trap moments before the explosion...too late. Cat's premonition seemed to have been accurate after all.

Cat...*where was she?* She was the one to point out this place. Had she purposely led him into a trap? He shook his head and coughed some of the dust out of his lungs. He needed to clear his head and start thinking straight.

He eased into a sitting position and gingerly rubbed his arm, stretching his legs experimentally. He did not appear to have broken any bones. His head felt sore and when he touched it, his hand came away sticky with blood. Also, his chest hurt. He gave a mental shrug. It could have been worse. He was still alive...he was still breathing. He looked around, trying to make out objects in the choking dust and smoke. He would try to stand in a minute, when his head stopped throbbing and he had a chance to evaluate his injuries.

He leaned against something hard and very uncomfortable. A mass of stones and rubble dug into his shoulders and back. Obviously, part of the building had collapsed, although most of it seemed to be still intact. Where the hell was Cat? She should not be far away. He'd dragged her off the staircase, and damn her if she'd led him into a trap and made a run for it. Could she be more involved with the Union than she wanted him to believe? Was that why her attitude toward him appeared so hostile, despite having probably saved his life yesterday?

He passed a hand across his eyes. Why would she risk her own safety by taking care of him when he was injured, only to lead him into a death trap? It made no sense.

He dislodged the pile of dust and debris that covered him, and used the pile of rubble behind him as support to help him stand. He rubbed his head again. He was going to have the mother and father of all headaches if he didn't do something about it soon. He needed to get out of here quickly. Clouds of thick, oleaginous smoke billowed around him accompanied by a heavy, acrid smell. He knew the place could erupt into flames at any moment, or be rocked by another explosion.

The device seemed to have gone off from somewhere at the top and toward the back of the building, or the damage to this part of the structure would have been worse. The door lay where it fell after he kicked it down earlier, twisted at a crazy angle, and the air from outside wafted in to dissipate some of the smoke. Even so, his eyes smarted and a paroxysm of coughing caused the muscles of his chest to protest and send a burning pain through his body. He'd probably sustained a couple of cracked ribs as well. He turned when he reached the doorway, as a soft moan reached his ears. He stopped and listened. Was it his imagination? No, there it was again.

Cat! She had not escaped the building after all. He tried to peer back through the smoke, and activated his wrist flare. Miraculously, it still worked. He flashed it around and called out softly. An answering groan came from somewhere near the stairs. Then he saw her. She lay trapped, almost completely buried beneath the shattered staircase and a pile of rubble. A wooden beam lay across her legs.

She groaned again, as he reached her, and in the light of his flare, her face shone pale as a corpse, streaked with blood and dirt, a smear of blood also on her lips. Her eyes flickered open, wide with pain. Dirt and rubble slid down the wall behind her and the building seemed to shudder. At any moment, the whole building could collapse.

"G-go," she whispered between low, rasping breaths. "Get away from here…as far away…as you can."

Chapter Five

"I'll not leave you here." Kerry grasped the beam with both his gloved hands and tried to move it away from her, giving an involuntary gasp as pain shot through him. Wedged fast, the beam did not budge. Wincing, he delved into his survival pack. The pain in his chest made breathing difficult. He would not be much help to her if he did not help himself first.

He flicked open the sealed pocket, thankful to find the regenerator undamaged. He activated it and ran it over his rib area, breathing deeply, and forcing himself to relax, then repeated the process on the gash on his head. After a few minutes, his body's healing processes repaired the damage and he took his small laser cutter and applied it to the wooden beam. At last, it split in two. He heaved each piece out of the way and shovelled away the stones and rubble with his hands.

He worked quickly. There was no time to be careful or cautious about injuring her further. He had to get them both out of there as soon as possible, before the rest of the building collapsed on top of them.

When at last he removed the detritus and stones that half buried her, he lifted her into his arms, forcing himself to ignore her half-stifled scream. She seemed to have some trouble breathing and must be in incredible pain. Certainly her ribs would be broken and probably one or both her legs. He hoped her spine wasn't injured or her lungs punctured, or moving her might kill or permanently maim her. What alternative did he have? To give her any chance of survival, he needed to get her out of here to somewhere safe where he could tend to her injuries.

He was scarcely more than a few hundred meters from the building, when a rumble like thunder shook the ground beneath him. He flung himself sideways to the ground, protecting Cat with his own body, and cast a glance over his shoulder. The whole side and roof of the structure had collapsed. A few minutes more and they would have been buried beneath it.

When he eventually reached a sheltered spot beneath some trees, encroaching dusk already made it difficult to see and he needed to use his flare to check the safety of the area. He laid Cat's unconscious body on the short, leafy vegetation beneath one of the largest trees, and put her survival pack beneath her head for a pillow. He removed his gloves and took a silver thermal blanket from his own pack. He tucked the blanket around her, and listened to her breathing. It sounded shallow and rasping. He placed a hand on her forehead. Her skin felt clammy and cold. If he didn't act quickly, she could go into shock and even the bio-regenerator might not be able to repair the damage in time.

He activated the instrument on the highest setting. The front of Cat's tunic was torn and bloodstained. He ripped it open to reveal a flimsy undergarment barely covering the swell of her full, firm breasts. He took a deep breath as unexpected heat coursed through his blood, and forced himself to ignore the feelings of arousal that stirred in his groin. He needed to concentrate on the task in hand if he was to have any chance of saving her.

Something compelled him to respect her privacy and not remove the garment. The regenerator normally worked through thin fabric, unless woven of metallic thread. Blood and livid black and purple bruises covered much of her upper body, marring the smooth skin, and he could only hope she'd not sustained any internal damage.

Thankfully, the charge was good and the instrument did its work. To his relief the initial scan registered no internal injury; the blood on her lips came from lacerations to her face. The healing process initiated by the regenerator would repair her leg, broken where the beam struck it, together with the broken ribs. Indications were that the rest of her injuries were not as bad as they looked.

Within a few minutes of initializing the regenerator, a faint flush tinged the deathly gray pallor of her skin. She was not out of the woods. He knew she must have lost a great deal of blood and it would take time, along with a few more treatments of the regenerator, for her to make it up. The situation bore similarities to when Zeldra was injured and Jon decided she needed to return to the *Destiny* where the ship's sophisticated medical facilities could ensure her rapid recovery. If he could only get Cat to the ship, her chances of survival would greatly increase.

He activated his communicator, and gave an urgent command but received nothing but static. Then Cat moaned and her eyes fluttered open.

"Lie still," he ordered. "Don't try to move. Are you in pain?"

"My leg hurts…and my chest."

"There was an explosion. You were hurt. I've used the regenerator, and your body is healing itself but it will take time. The pain should ease soon, but you are weak from lack of blood."

"Am...am I going to die?" He had to admire her courage. Her voice held a hint of curiosity, rather than fear.

"Not if I can help it," he promised. "I will try to raise the *Destiny* and get you to her sickbay, if I can make contact."

"And if not..."

"Then you are going to have me as a nursemaid for a while. Now be quiet and rest."

"What about...Shifter?"

Kerry had forgotten about the animal. "He's fine. He is around somewhere," he lied. The last thing she needed was to become stressed worrying about the animal. "He is probably foraging for food. Lie still and try to get some sleep while I fix something to eat."

"Promise me...you'll take care of him...if I don't...make it."

She lay back and closed her eyes.

"You'll make it," he growled, and debated whether there was time to get her back to her escape vessel before night fell. He decided against it. She needed to rest. Forcing her to move would delay her recovery, and with darkness closing in fast, carrying her would be doubly difficult and dangerous.

The thermal blanket would reflect every bit of warmth back to her body, diminishing the risk of hypothermia. Thank the stars they still possessed their survival packs. At least they would not starve, and the water containers should keep them going until they got back to her craft. He tried several times to contact the *Destiny* with no response. Eventually, he decided he was just wasting his communicator's power.

He used a little of their precious water to wipe the dirt and grime from her face. A quick scan of the area indicated the presence of a river nearby, but for tonight, they would have to manage with what they had. He would not risk leaving her alone, when there could be countless unknown dangers lurking in the twilight. His bio-scanner registered no nearby lifeforms, but recently, too many things had happened that could not be accounted for. He did not intend to take any chances.

Cat dozed for a time, and he ran the bio-regenerator over her face on the lowest setting to speed the healing of the remaining bruises and cuts. After a while, she opened her eyes and ran her tongue over her cracked lips.

He took the flask of water and held it to her mouth. After choking a little, she drank and the ghost of a smile crossed her face.

"Thought I was going to die for a while there."

"No chance. I have some questions I need to ask you when you have recovered enough. There was no way I would let you die and leave them unanswered."

She smiled again, a smile without warmth or humour, as if she knew something she was determined to keep secret, and closed her eyes. In repose, the lines of her face softened, transforming her from the strong, hard-headed woman who'd threatened him, to a woman he grudgingly admitted was rather more than attractive, even with her clothes torn and bloodied, and covered in dirt. The auburn hair hung loose, framing her face, reminding him even more of…he shook his head. He could still not be sure where her allegiance lay. Besides, they could be under attack from unknown assailants at any moment. This was not the time to be getting sentimental.

He busied himself with the survival rations. A self-heating canister of what passed for chicken soup, in reality, a protein and vitamin compound, should help build her strength.

When the contents of the container heated through, he allowed the broth to cool enough so as not to burn her lips and supported her head as she sipped, slowly at first and then with more relish.

"How do you feel now?"

She gave a wry smile. "I have to admit I've felt better."

"You are lucky to be alive at all."

"I suppose so. The tables seem to have turned. Now I owe *you*."

"I would say we're even. You took care of me when I was hurt. The least I could do was return the favour." He allowed himself a humourless smile. "Now we can try to kill each other with a clear conscience."

Cat closed her eyes. She would probably not need the light sleeping draft he'd slipped into the soup, but it would do no harm. At least if she slept, her body would have chance to continue healing and make up the blood she'd lost, and she would be out of pain. He would run the bio-regenerator over her again as soon as he knew she was asleep.

His main problem now would be to stay awake himself. He needed to try to figure out exactly what was going on. And why someone on this planet appeared determined to kill them both.

Chapter Six

Darkness descended like a heavy, enveloping cloak over the brooding landscape, bringing with it nothing but silence. Kerry again used the bio-regenerator on Cat. It could be dangerous to use it too often, but her injuries were serious enough to require the highest dose of treatment he could safely administer.

The air felt less chilled than on the previous night, and the wind had changed direction, away from their present location, so he decided not to erect his small tent. It would mean moving Cat again, and he preferred not to disturb her, the thermal blanket should keep her warm enough. Building a fire would be too risky as well. Whoever booby-trapped the building might still be out there somewhere, and any smoke or glow in the darkness would tell them exactly where to find their target.

Fortunately, he did not need a lot of sleep. A few hours normally sufficed. Just as well because he could not allow himself the luxury of even closing his eyes tonight.

Digging out a spare jacket from his pack, he allowed it to decompress before wrapping it around his shoulders and leaning against the tree beneath which Cat slept. The night dragged on, seemingly interminable. He gazed up at the sky. A few stray wisps of cloud drifted across, partially obscuring the three distant moons, and making their dim light seem ethereal. He tried to reconcile the unfamiliar constellations with the star maps the *Destiny's* computer, *Metisa,* projected on their screens before he and the others made planetfall.

A meteor shot across the sky, its bright glory lasting for only a moment, before it burned up in the atmosphere. He sighed as once more the memories drifted in. Memories he usually managed to keep hidden in the secret recesses of his mind—hidden like the bitter tears he wept in the lonely privacy of his cabin on board the *Destiny*. Recollections of another time, another planet...and Jess who loved the stars so much. Jess, whose faith never wavered, and yet whose God allowed her to die so young, when it should have been him. He ran his hand across his face, in his mind seeing her seated before the observation screen on the *Destiny,* as she watched the stars and planets in the vastness of deep space. Entranced by their beauty, she tried to convince him that such beauty could not be the result of a mere cosmic accident. He sighed as he recalled her soft, husky voice telling him about her childhood on Earth. How, with her mother, she used to watch the night sky for falling stars.

A moan, followed by words he could not quite make out, interrupted his reverie. He looked toward Cat. She turned restlessly, her arms flung out. She must be having a nightmare. He went over to where she lay and laid his hand on her forehead. Her skin was warm, but not hot. There was no fever. After a few moments, her movements quietened, and her breathing became steady again. He pulled back the thermal blanket, adjusted the regenerator settings, and swiftly ran the instrument over her sleeping form. It registered her life signs as normal. Her body must have made up the loss of blood and completed the healing process. He pulled the blanket back over her once more. She looked so innocent and calm when asleep, almost vulnerable. But it was an illusion. She gave the impression of being a killer, and he could imagine she would be ruthless in a tight corner. Although, he had to admit, he could be pretty ruthless himself. In space, it came with the territory.

If her story about the crew of her ship being androids was true, that might excuse her making a getaway when she could. Nevertheless, directly or indirectly, she worked for the Union, the same Global and planetary authority whose corrupt policies caused him and the *Destiny*'s crew to leave Earth, so long ago.

Reports of the Union's ruthless actions spread across the galaxy. They were disturbing— assassinations, so-called "executions" of anyone who stood in their way, and a relentless advance across uncharted space, capturing every world in their path.

Although Cat denied working for the Union, she wore their insignia. And she'd admitted to capturing ships for them. So, despite their agreement, he questioned the wisdom of even allowing her on board the *Destiny* once he managed to contact the rest of the crew. He'd given her his word, and had every intention of keeping it, if he could, but his first loyalty would always be to the *Destiny* and her crew.

She cried out again, more loudly. Her eyes were wide open now, staring ahead. "No…no," she gasped and flung her arms out.

"Stay still," Kerry hissed. "Stay still and save your

energy." He grasped her outstretched hand to stop her flinging off the blanket. "What's up? Were you having a nightmare?"

"I…I dreamt I was buried beneath a pile of stones. It was dark, so dark. I couldn't breathe."

"Part of the walls of the building collapsed and fell on us in the explosion. You're safe now. We are well away from there."

"I thought…I thought we were trapped. I'm not afraid of dying…but not like that…not buried alive."

"Are you still in pain? You should not be. The regenerator should have taken care of that."

"No, I don't think so…but it's night. I can see the moons." She tried to rise. "Have you slept at all?"

"Someone has to keep watch. Whoever planted the explosive device did it for a reason. They might decide to come back and finish the job."

"We should take turns…"

"Don't talk like an idiot. You are in no fit condition. Go back to sleep. You will need to be fit enough to travel tomorrow."

Somewhat to his surprise, she did not argue, and within minutes, her even breathing told him she slept again. He realized his hand still grasped hers. He tried to remove it without disturbing her, but she moaned again and clutched his fingers. Something stirred deep within him, something he had vowed never to experience again. He forced himself to vanquish the unexpected and unbidden wave of desire, tenderness even, that threatened the virtual force field he'd built around his heart. After Jess's death, he'd vowed he would never again get close to another woman—to protect himself from the possibility of ever again descending into the morass of despair he felt then, the grief he'd never really come to terms with, and his inability to move beyond those feelings.

This woman, so much like Jess in some ways, and so very different in others, was his enemy. Whether she admitted it or not, she evidently worked for a corrupt regime, and he would not ally himself with it—or her.

\*\*\*\*

Cat awoke to the faint glow of approaching dawn across the hills to the far side of an otherwise featureless landscape. The moons still shone, although most of the stars glimmered as faint ghosts, apart from one or two particularly bright planets. She took a deep breath. The technology of Kerry's regenerator had undoubtedly saved her life. She tried to erase the memory of being buried under piles of rubble. The recollections that invaded her sleep as a nightmare and even now, with dawn chasing away the darkness, made her shudder and try to block the images in her head.

It was a miracle she was still alive. She knew it would have been a different story if it wasn't for the man sitting as still as a rock beside her, his blaster laid on his knee, one hand on the weapon, and the other lying on top of her own. A vague recollection of him taking hold of her hand last night filtered into her mind. Was it to comfort her…or to restrain her? He didn't seem like the kind of man who would perform such an act of gentleness.

She found herself observing his face or what she could see of it in profile; handsome and rugged with a firm chin and long, aristocratic nose. She could not see his eyes from this angle, but the image of them burned into her mind—a deep, almost metallic blue with a distant, haunted expression in their depths. Eyes that would sear into one's soul, without giving anything of themselves away.

As if feeling her gaze upon him, he removed his hand and turned to look at her.

"It will be morning soon. Do you think you will be fit to travel?"

"I feel fine. Why don't you get some rest, and I'll stand watch?"

"I don't need to rest. We will need to get moving in a few hours."

"If you're suffering from sleep deprivation, you won't be a lot of use to either of us. There must be a few hours before dawn yet. Go on. Get some rest. I promise I won't shoot you while you sleep."

He rewarded her with that brilliant and all too rare smile. "How comforting. Just be sure to wake me if there is the slightest hint of anything unusual."

"Where's my gun?"

"Here." He handed over her holster. "I had to remove it when you were injured. It appears to be in working order. Your pack is serving as your pillow."

She nodded. He'd probably made a thorough inspection of her weapon. No doubt, he'd examined it in minute detail and taken note of the specific alterations she'd made.

Kerry slept while still sitting, his blaster across his knees, as before, his hand on the barrel. He must be tired, but it was typical of the man she was coming to know to refuse to show any sign of weakness, by not allowing himself to lie down to sleep in comfort. It would not surprise her if he waited until daybreak to close his eyes.

She realized she'd not seen Shifter since she regained consciousness. She'd been so out of it the night before, she'd hardly given him a thought, although she vaguely remembered asking about him, and some sort of non-committal response from Kerry. What if he'd been injured, or killed in the explosion? Kerry hadn't mentioned him this morning. Did that mean the animal was missing—or dead—and he didn't want to tell her? Surely not. He wouldn't be so sensitive to her feelings would he? Everything about him seemed to indicate he was a man who didn't deal in sentiment. Surely, he'd have told her straight out if anything had happened to Shifter.

She walked a little way away from their makeshift camp and peered into the semi-darkness. It would be foolish to wander too far, but she needed to know Shifter was all right. She fumbled in the pocket of her slacks and activated a small audio device. Like the whistles dog trainers on Earth used for centuries, the high frequency did not register with human ears, but if the animal was around, he would hear it and respond.

After a few minutes, she tried again, and eventually, to her relief, a patch of vegetation moved and revealed itself to be the chameleopard.

The creature loped up to her, and she bent to stroke his head. "There you are, Shifter, you big lunk. I was afraid something happened to you. Where've you been? Off hunting, I guess." She turned back with the animal at her heels.

By the time the sun rose high enough in the sky to be able to see across the plain, she'd already prepared breakfast from their supplies. Her blood encrusted tunic hung about her in tatters. She removed it and donned one of the two spares she carried in her pack—one without the Union insignia. She buried the torn one beneath a spiny plant in the soft, ochre-coloured dirt, a short distance from the camp. There was no way it could be mended. Besides the blood, the material was ripped down the front. Obviously, Kerry had needed to get past the material to use the bio-regenerator. The idea of him removing her outer garment caused her breath to catch and the back of her neck to tingle. If she were the type to blush, she would have sworn she felt her skin burn. Perhaps it was just as well she'd been unconscious.

Thank the stars she always carried some spare clothing in her pack. Her slacks were more jagged holes than fabric. She pulled on a pair of tough, form hugging leggings, tucked the hem of her tunic inside the waistband, and fastened her belt. She could not find the scarf she used to keep back her hair. It probably lay buried in the rubble of the old building. Although there should be a couple more in her pack, for the moment, she merely ran a comb through the tangled mass and made a thick braid, knotting the end to keep it in place. She rubbed her face with her hand. She would be very glad when she could wash away the dirt. Her skin felt as though it were encrusted with several layers of dust and dried mud.

She glanced toward the tree where she last saw Kerry. There was no sign of him. A feeling of alarm welled up in her. Where was he?

It wasn't as if she'd never faced being alone on a strange planet before. Even though still weak from her injuries of the previous day, she could cope perfectly well with anything, or anyone, who confronted her.

Still, despite her reservations, she'd grown used to him being there, and two people were safer than one alone.

While the thought still formulated in her mind, he reappeared from somewhere to her left, like a shadow emerging from a dark corner.

"There is still no answer from my ship. Something could have caused her to go into hyperspace, although solar activity is still the most likely explanation. As I said, if she had been destroyed, we would know about it."

"What makes you speak about her being destroyed? Was she in danger?"

"Not that I am aware of," Kerry said in measured tones. "However, something is preventing us from making contact, and I'm starting to think it is something more than solar disturbances." He glanced toward the chameleopard. "I see the wolf came back."

"Yes, and he's not a wolf. In fact, if anything, he's related more to a big cat if you want to compare him to Terran animals."

"He still looks like a wolf to me."

"We need to eat." She nodded toward the containers of food she'd laid out for breakfast. He squatted beside her and neither of them spoke while they ate their meagre rations.

"How long will your shield hold out?"

"Indefinitely, so long as there's no sudden power drain, and I can't think of any reason why there would be. It should absorb enough power from the sun to keep going."

"Then we can assume it will be safe enough to use your vehicle as a base."

"It's either that or try to find the nearest settlement.

And after yesterday's incident, I'm not sure that's such a good idea." She paused. "That bio-regenerator of yours is an amazing piece of equipment. I don't quite understand why your companion needed to be taken to your ship."

"It is an excellent tool, but it does have its limitations. Zeldra lost so much blood she needed to have an immediate transfusion. The regenerator enhances the body's natural healing processes, but it can't cope with such a huge blood loss. I only hope they made it to the ship in time."

His voice held no trace of emotion, but she caught a hint of concern in his eyes although his expression remained impassive.

"Luckily for you," he went on, "although your injuries were serious, you appear not to have lost as much blood as I feared and the regenerator treatment was sufficient. Now, since you seem to be recovered, let's get back to your vessel."

****

Anxious not to waste the daylight, they cleared away the evidence of their meal and started on the return journey to the escape craft. After walking for some time, they reached the beginning of the incline, but at the edge of the downslope, they stopped and exchanged glances.

In what should be an empty space in the clearing, some distance away from the thicket where she crashed her escape vehicle, sat a large hyper speedster. The branches and shrubbery had been hacked down, and a large part of her escape vehicle was now visible. Several figures in uniform moved along the hull of the craft, apparently giving it close inspection. She recognized those uniforms, and looking at the furrow on Kerry's brow and the intent expression in his eyes, she knew they were familiar to him, too.

Kerry threw himself down on his stomach, and Cat followed suit. If one of the people down there looked up, they'd be sitting targets. Her tri-dee-viewer lay buried at the bottom of her emergency pack. She'd put it there when she changed her tunic that morning, meaning to hang it in its usual place around her neck. She looked across and saw Kerry already using his. Wordlessly, he handed it across to her. She peered at the screen and adjusted the focus.

She squinted, made another adjustment, and concentrated the instrument on two figures that stood a little apart from the others. She drew in a sharp, incredulous breath.

*It couldn't be—the last person she expected or ever wanted to see again.*

Chapter Seven

What was he doing here, now, on this planet? Did he know this was her escape craft? And what about the woman with him? She made another adjustment and focused on the two figures again. The woman wore her dark hair short in an almost masculine style. Her perfectly tailored uniform moulded to her figure as if she were dressed for a parade. She and the man next to her seemed to be in charge over the others. There was something familiar about her general height and build, the self-assured way she held herself, but she stood with her back to her and Kerry and did not turn to give a clear view of her face. She held a small device aimed in the direction of Cat's escape vessel.

She handed the viewer back to Kerry, and he gave her an enquiring look. She tried to keep her expression impassive. She hadn't thought of Dorian for a long time, and she didn't particularly want to talk about him now. Kerry gave a curt nod, indicating they should retreat to some cover, well out of sight of the figures below.

"The Global Union," Kerry breathed as they crouched in the undergrowth. "It seems they either traced your distress signal, or the signature given off by your escape craft when it crashed." His eyes flashed with suspicion as he held her gaze with his own. "Unless you sent a signal to them while I slept."

"Of course not." Cat did not hide the resentment in her voice. "Looks like we can forget going back to it until they leave."

"They are not friends of yours?"

She shook her head and scowled at him. "No, they're not."

"Strange, I had the feeling you recognized someone down there." When she made no answer, he went on, "I wonder how many of them are here. This could be just an isolated scouting expedition, or it could be the advance party for a wholesale invasion." He gave her a hard look, eyes narrowed. "You must have some idea of what they are up to."

"What makes you think I know any more about their motives than you do?"

"You work for them don't you? Why not just go down there and ask them?"

"It's really not that simple."

He gave her another of his scathing looks. "I bet it's not. We need to get out of here. They appear to be armed to the hilt, and I don't fancy staying around to find out what their intentions are."

"Neither do I."

They retreated until they were a safe distance away. All at once, Kerry stopped and, following close behind, she almost ran into him.

"I am going to make another attempt at contacting the *Destiny*," he said, "and then we can discuss what our next move is."

He spoke into his communicator, and after several attempts, turned away in exasperation. "Still nothing. Any suggestions?"

"From what I saw, it looks like since they couldn't

get past my craft's shield, they've decided to set a trap by putting an electronic cordon around it. So we're not going to be able to get into it any time soon."

"Tell me something I don't already know." He gave her another searching look. "Why would they do that anyway? What are you hiding?"

She shrugged and looked at him in exasperation "How should I know? And I'm not hiding anything."

"There is little point in lying to each other," he said in the soft tone she recognized as a sign he was losing patience. "Like it or not, it looks like we are going to have to work together if we are ever going to get off this planet."

He was right, hard though it was to admit. Together they stood a much better chance of survival than if they tried to make it alone. Perhaps she should tell him about Dorian.

"You know one of those people down there, don't you?" he asked, as if reading her mind.

"Yes, we go back a long way."

"Is he the reason why you don't want to go down there and ask them why the hell they are trying to prevent you from getting to your escape craft?"

She knew he was curious about her relationship with the Union Officer, but wasn't prepared to go into details, especially not with him. Not this man—a man she'd sworn vengeance upon—who was somehow so disturbing. "Partly." She shivered, and glanced at the darkening sky, noticing for the first time clouds building up and the gradual sharpening of the wind.

He frowned. "You're cold? We need to find some shelter. It looks like there is a storm brewing, and you've barely recovered from yesterday."

"I'm fine. You don't need to worry about me."

"No?" For a moment, the contours of his face appeared to soften.

"We're even, remember?" she said, thrown of balance. "You don't owe me anything."

"I was not aware we were trading favours."

Why did his sudden apparent concern for her seem to hit such a raw nerve? Was it merely the fact no one had expressed concern over her for so long she felt she no longer needed it? No, she didn't need anyone's pity. So why did the hairs on her neck stand up and her heart seem to leap into her throat as he drew closer—so close she could feel his breath on her face as his relentless gaze held her own.

She took a step back, forcing herself to keep eye contact. She would not give him any advantage by dropping her gaze. "You said you had questions you wanted to ask," she said. "I have a few of my own."

The cerulean eyes, previously so cold, gazed even deeper into hers, piercing, searching. "Yes. We have more than a little in common, I think."

"I don't know what you mean."

"Oh, but I think you do. It seems to me that we both have things and people in the past we wish we could forget—ghosts we need to exorcise."

She took a deep breath and forced herself to break his hypnotic gaze. She couldn't think clearly when he looked at her that way. She silently cursed her own weakness. She would not allow any man to have a hold on her again. The important thing at the moment was to get off this planet. After that, she needed to find out what happened to her sister and avenge her death. Perhaps then, she could think about exorcising those ghosts.

Kerry's expression hardened once more. "Not now, though. There will be time enough for questions later. We need to get away from here."

"Suits me." She turned and gave a low call, and Shifter materialized once more and padded behind them like a dog.

"Let's head back to our old camp. It will do as a temporary base while we decide what to do next. We can set up a shelter and the river is not far away. The water is safe. I tested it this morning, before I tried to contact the *Destiny* again."

She kept a keen lookout for any signs of potential trouble as they walked, and noticed how Kerry constantly looked around him too. Shifter would doubtless warn her of any sign of danger, but there was no sense in taking any chances.

Kerry's face set in its usual expressionless lines. Although he usually hid it well, she could read the lines of worry on his face, and the grief never faded from his eyes. He was obviously not ready to share with her yet—not any more than she felt ready to talk about Dorian. He must be worried about his ship. Why had he not been able to contact the *Destiny* for so long? Presumably, if his two companions had managed to get back on board, they would surely have made contact by now, unless he was right about solar flare activity blocking the signal.

"We need to move a little closer to the river," Kerry said, when they reached the spot where they'd pitched camp the night before. "I had to stop as soon as I found a suitable place yesterday, in order to treat you quickly. Otherwise, it might have been too late. There is no reason not to make a more convenient camp now though."

"I suppose it's not safe to build a campfire," Cat said. "There's no point in taking risks and giving our position away."

"I have several heat and light globes in my pack. We didn't need them last night, but it looks like there is a storm brewing. I have a small tent in my pack as well."

"You're better equipped than I am. I just grabbed the basic necessities when I escaped in my transit vehicle."

"Then we'll have to share mine, although it will be a bit cramped."

"Fine, I'm sure we'll manage," she muttered. The idea of being in close proximity to him no longer seemed so abhorrent, and they'd been close enough last night.

In the time she took to think about it, he took the compressed tent out of his pack and set it up. He was right. It was small, but it would suffice. Besides, they'd need to take turns on watch through the night, so the question of sleeping next to each other would not arise.

Thunder rumbled in the distance, and the first drops of rain began to fall.

"Looks like we only just got set up in time. Damn this storm though, I wanted to have another try at contacting the *Destiny*. Pointless now with all this electrical interference in the atmosphere."

"It might not last too long. You can try later," she said, realizing how lame her attempt of reassurance sounded.

They ate an uncomfortable meal while the rain

poured down outside. The chameleopard disappeared at the first clap of thunder. "He'll dig a hole in the ground and hide there until the storm's over," she told Kerry when he queried the animal's disappearance. "He'll be fine. We've been through storms together before."

By the time they finished eating, the pounding rain had quietened to a steady drizzle. "I'll take first watch," Kerry said, ignoring her protests. "Get some sleep. You will be more alert to danger when you've rested, since you are still getting over your injuries."

She wished he wouldn't keep reminding her. She drew in a deep breath, shrugging her shoulders in resignation. No point in arguing with a man as stubborn as herself.

****

Kerry sat just inside the perimeter of the tent. It provided enough shelter to keep him from getting too wet, so long as the wind did not blow directly toward him. He utilized one of the light globes from his pack and placed it on one side, just inside the doorway. Its light rendered enough illumination for him to watch for any intruders and also provided a little warmth. It could be deactivated in a second if necessary, and its soft glow should not carry far enough to attract attention. Ironically, extra light was hardly necessary at the moment. Frequent lightning flashes lit up the surrounding countryside for miles around.

His mind, never inactive, teemed with jumbled thoughts and questions. His failure to contact the *Destiny* worried him more than a little. There must be something radically wrong for her not to have been either contactable, or in touch with him. Once the storm abated, he would try again.

The woman sleeping in close proximity, just behind him, filled his thoughts more than he cared to admit. He still could not be sure which side she was actually on. He would have expected her to approach the Union personnel, since she admitted to privateering for them, but she seemed very keen to avoid them seeing her. What was she up to? Perhaps she had double-crossed them for purposes of her own. If so, she probably deserved whatever they meted out if they caught her, and she was either very courageous or very stupid. Somehow, he did not believe her to be the latter.

He squinted into the distance. He knew enough about the Union's methods to be sure he would not wish them on any human being. Hadn't he and Jon built the *Destiny* to get away from the tyranny of the Global Union in the first place? There was something about Cat's manner though. She admitted to recognizing one of the Union personnel, so why her reluctance to explain who he was? What else was she hiding from him?

The rain stopped as suddenly as it started, and the thunder now only rumbled in the distance, the worst of the storm having abated. His keen hearing discerned the slight rustle of something creeping through the sparse undergrowth. A shadow moved in the darkness. He aimed his blaster in the direction of the sound.

The shadow melted into a long, wolf like form. He relaxed as Shifter poked his head past him and sniffed, then as if satisfied of his mistress's safety, lay down and rested his large head on his paws. Absently Kerry stroked the creature's head. He'd never had an opportunity to keep a pet himself, but perhaps relying on the companionship of an animal might be a lot simpler than trying to understand human nature and relationships.

****

Cat woke with a start and reached instinctively for the handgun she'd tucked under her blanket.

"Relax, it's only me. It is your turn for watch. I have some hot coffee brewed if you want it."

She sat up and took the proffered cup. "Thanks. Any sign of…anything?"

"No, it's quite peaceful out there. Shifter came back, and it has stopped raining."

"Good. You'd better get some rest then, I'll take over."

She took up the position Kerry vacated by the entrance to the tent. She'd slept deeply with no dreams. Just as well. She feared a certain Dorian Krell would invade her sleep, but she was more tired than she realized, and slept solidly until Kerry woke her.

The chameleopard stretched out beside her. The animal served as more than just a comfort. If anyone or anything approached within a few meters, he'd attack on command, and with his size and strength could down an average sized man with ease. Nevertheless, she kept a firm grip on her pistol. She wasn't about to take any chances.

She glanced back over her shoulder at the sleeping form of Kerry, vaguely visible in the faint light of the globe. She could not be sure if he really slept or not, and could not shake off the sensation he might be watching her even though his eyes looked closed. Quickly, she turned back. *Ignore him. Don't let him get to you.* She hoped he'd be able to contact his ship once daybreak came. Surely, they wouldn't have deserted him? As he'd said, if anything catastrophic had happened to the *Destiny,* there would almost certainly be some evidence. However, it was obvious the lack of contact bothered him more than he let on.

What would be her fate when the ship did eventually make contact? If she told them the truth, would they hand her over to the Union? She knew Kerry harboured no love for the regime, but how did the others on the *Destiny* feel? Supposing none of them believed her, or just decided to hand her over anyway? If the Union knew about the *chip*, there might even be a bounty out on her head. Either way she knew her chances were not good. Perhaps it would be better to sneak off with Shifter and try to survive alone. She had nothing to lose—did she? She might eventually find a settlement whose inhabitants were a little more friendly than whoever had laid the booby trap that so nearly killed them both.

She stole another glance over her shoulder toward him. He seemed to be fully asleep now, the sound of his steady breathing the only thing to break the silence. The man intrigued her. She would love to know the identity of the woman in the locket. Had the tiny gold cross belonged to her as well? She could not help a wry grin. She could be pretty certain he was as intrigued about her. They seemed to have that, at least, in common.

****

Kerry joined her before the sun rose fully in the sky. He sat next to her and they shared their rations. Cat looked out over the landscape. After the previous night's storm, the land looked fresher and much greener. Clumps of unfamiliar and outlandish flowers, sprung up after the rain, made bright splashes of colour on the formerly dull gray-brown expanse. Vibrant red, yellow, and orange hues and here and there a patch of deep blue. Even the air smelt fresher, the ever-present breeze cooler now bearing scents of damp vegetation and exotic flora.

Rays of early sunlight bounced off the river, illuminating the water in shades of pink and molten gold, causing it to sparkle like gemstones. Calm and crystal clear the night before, the river moved much more swiftly now, its surface covered with white flecks of foam. Kerry walked to its edge and filled the water containers for their emergency packs.

She looked upstream, to where it widened out into a deep pool. The water called to her. The slap-slap of the waves against the bank and the swoosh of the water racing past invited her in. She'd had no opportunity to remove the dust and grime from her body since the explosion that nearly took her life. She shuddered inwardly. It would have done so, and she wouldn't be here now, if it wasn't for this quiet, sullen man who would have killed her himself if she made one wrong move.

"I'd give anything to bathe in that pool."

He studied her, his lips twitching at the corners. "For all we know there are Union personnel in the vicinity whom it seems we would both prefer to avoid—and you want to bathe?"

"All right. It was just a suggestion. We're in danger of running into them whether we stay here or move on. If we're going to get killed, I'd prefer to die clean."

Kerry gave her one of those smiles that had such a disturbing effect on her. "I suppose you have a point. I'm going to attempt to contact the *Destiny* again. Then you can bathe while I put the tent and supplies away."

He repeated the process she'd watched him go through so many times. After the third attempt to get some response from his communicator, he cursed, and looked at her, his face expressionless, but concern showing in his eyes.

"I can only assume it *is* solar flare interference. Our computer did indicate some greater than usual solar activity. I will just have to keep trying until it subsides."

"Well, I'm going to wash away some of this grime. I'm taking this with me." She indicated her handgun. "Just in case."

"There is no need to worry, I won't look. I have other things on my mind."

"Don't flatter yourself. It's the Union I'm concerned about."

Cat went a few hundred meters upstream, where some overhanging branches hid her from view, or so she hoped. She tossed a few pebbles into the water. Nothing. Okay, she'd take a chance and hope there weren't any undesirable life forms in the depths. The current didn't seem too strong, and the water ran crystal clear. Silver shoals of small fish flashed beneath the surface. Presumable they wouldn't be around if there were predators lurking in the water. She would stay near the bank though, so she could scramble out quickly if necessary.

She stripped off her clothes and after removing a small container of concentrated liquid soap from her pack, waded in until the water reached halfway up her breasts. The coldness of the water initially made her gasp, but after a few seconds, she became acclimatized to it. If today followed the usual pattern, the heat of the sun would soon be almost unbearable and the river would warm up, but now the water was cool and invigorating. She'd un-braided her hair and shaken out as much of the dirt and dust as she could before she went to sleep the previous night, but it needed a good wash. She ducked beneath the water several times and rubbed her head briskly, using some of the plant based soap. It felt good to be able to wash the dirt off her body and after some more brisk rubbing, her hair felt clean again. She untangled the knots with her fingers, unable to avoid breaking off few strands in the process, and gave it another rinse.

While she washed, she kept her gaze on her pistol laid at the base the tree. Despite her sarcastic comment to the contrary, she hoped her hinted warning would deter Kerry from following her. Her main concern though, was that a wild animal, or even worse, a Union patrol might creep up on her unexpectedly. She did not indulge in the refreshing qualities of the water any longer than necessary. She wrung the water from her hair and shook her head so the thick mane swirled around her shoulders. It would soon dry in the warm wind. She sat on the grass and rubbed her skin with her hands trying to remove as much moisture as she could before donning her clothes once more. At least, she felt cleaner and fresher now. She delved into her pack for a scarf, and after tying back her hair again, made her way back to the camp.

Kerry leaned against a spindly tree. He turned to look at her as she approached

"Your turn," she told him.

He regarded her with a slightly quizzical expression.

"You got just as dirty and dusty as I did when that building collapsed around us. I assume you'd like to wash some of the grime away?"

"I can take a hint." Again came the flashing smile that made her tremble at the knees and forget she'd sworn off men. "I assume I can rely on you not to peek?" He picked up his blaster and without another word made for the same spot in the stream that she recently vacated.

****

Kerry hated to admit it but Cat had a point. They'd had no chance to clean up after the explosion two days ago. The leather tunic and trousers he wore kept the worst of the dirt and dust from his skin but he did need a proper wash.

When Cat bathed earlier, it had taken a fair amount of willpower to avoid looking up stream. Once he glanced in her general direction and caught a teasing glimpse of naked skin and a flash of red in the sunlight as she shook her long hair. Even at that distance, with her back turned toward him, her slim, statuesque form made his body react in a way entirely inappropriate for the situation.

Although he'd dutifully looked away again, the memory remained stubbornly imprinted in his mind.

The shock as the cold water hit him came as something of a relief, bringing him back to reality. He washed himself quickly and thoroughly, and after scrubbing at the dirt and grime clinging to his arms and body, climbed back on the bank. He stretched out his arms and shook off some of the excess water. Pity he had nothing to dry himself with, but it should not take too long to dry off in the warmth of the sun.

He dug around in his pack for a change of clothing and was half dressed again when a rustle in the reeds and an almighty splash on the other side of the river made him reach for his blaster. A creature, which must have been all of five meters tall, surfaced out of the water on the opposite side of the river and plunged toward him.

## Chapter Eight

Kerry had come across some weird creatures in his travels, but nothing quite like this. A few yards from shore, it reared up, the water streaming over its body.

Gray-skinned, with short, bristly hairs covering its thorax, its elongated, pointed ears lay flat on its neck. Red eyes bulged in a head too small for its body, above a long narrow jaw with a double row of long, pointed teeth. It waved the upper part of its segmented body from side to side, like a monstrous caterpillar. Three pairs of arms with wicked looking pincers, and several pairs of tentacle-like appendages flailed the air. It opened its mouth and emitted a ground-shaking roar. Even at that distance, its fetid breath, like rancid fish, nearly made him choke.

He ducked and leapt to one side. The creature lunged, and a sharp talon raked him across his bare shoulder. He snatched his blaster from the riverbank where he'd laid it while he bathed. He touched the trigger button, but a blow from one of the tentacles landed him on his back and the blast went wild. He thanked his stars he'd pulled on his trousers and tough boots before it attacked, and kicked out hard, with both feet, impacting with the creature's soft underbelly and then letting loose the full force of the weapon's charge. The arthropod gave a blood-curdling, high-pitched shriek before leaping at him again. He flung himself out of the way and fired once more. He thought the shot went wide of its target again, but to his relief the air shimmered for a moment in the flare of an energy bolt, the creature gave another mind-shattering shriek, and fell backwards, sending up a spray of water.

He rose to his feet, running his hand across his arm and shoulder, where the monster's talons had torn through the skin.

"Just as well I was around to save your hide again." Cat stood, pistol drawn, surveying the water which now ran a sickly yellow green where the creature's blood seeped from the wound in its belly. She let loose another couple of plasma bolts as if to make sure.

He followed her gaze. "Thank you. I believe it's dead now."

She turned back to him. "Do you have your bio regenerator with you?"

"Of course." He felt around in his hip pocket for the instrument. "I can manage," he said, waving away the hand she held out. For a few moments, he ground his teeth against the burning, tingling sensation. Almost miraculously, the wounds closed and new skin grew over them, leaving him with nothing more than a slight tenderness where the claws raked his shoulder.

He bent to retrieve his tunic from the ground. "I hope that thing has no friends lurking around," he muttered, staring at the river for any signs of movement.

"I wonder how many more wild creatures are out there waiting for the chance to get an easy meal."

"I had no intention of making it 'easy'," he said, with the best approximation he could muster of a wry grin. Where had the monster come from? The water must be a lot deeper toward the far shore than it looked, to have concealed such a large animal.

"You'd better have an anti-toxin shot, when we get back to camp, just in case. No telling what might be in that animal's claws," Cat remarked. "I'm amazed it didn't do more damage. It was huge. I heard it and came running. For a moment, I thought I was too late."

"I admit I was a little concerned myself," he said, tucking the instrument back into his pocket and slipping his arm into the sleeve of his tunic. "As it was, the creature knocked me off my feet before I could get a shot—" The words froze on his lips, as he looked over her head to the river behind her, letting the tunic fall to the ground. He raised his blaster and yelled, "Out of the way—now!"

****

"Wha-at?" Cat flung herself sideways. Her feet slid from under her as something long and black wrapped itself round her leg, writhing and tightening its coils. She hit the ground hard, rolling over to her shoulder, almost deafened by the sound of Kerry's blaster. The water sprayed up from the river and her throat burned with the acrid smell of blaster emissions and burning flesh. Gravel and pebbles dug into her skin through the fabric of her clothing, as something dragged her toward the edge of the bank. She bit back a cry of horror as she glanced over her shoulder at the thing twining itself around her leg. An icy fear went through her. Snakes— the only creatures she really feared. She aimed her pistol and then realized it was not a serpent that dragged her toward the river, but a long, rubbery tentacle fastened around the tough material of her leggings and boot.

Before she could activate the weapon, Kerry let off another barrage of plasma bolts into the river. He leapt toward her and ripped the severed tentacle from her leg. It flapped around on the wet grass. She scrambled to her knees, still slightly winded, and fired at the hideous thing. The foliage around it flared briefly with an eerie green flame, and the tentacle shrivelled into a slimy black mass, emitting a pungent odour and causing her to gag.

"It seems I was mistaken about the creature being dead." Kerry prodded the smouldering mass with his boot and looked across over the water. "It is now." He leaned down and grasped her wrist to haul her to her feet. "Are you hurt?"

"No, I don't think so." Her shoulder was sore and probably bruised but she'd live.

She tried to control her shivering. The incident affected her more than she wanted to admit. Kerry's proximity—naked to the waist, his lithe body shining from the water droplets that still clung to his skin, and his legs swathed in tight black leather—did nothing to help. The last thing she wanted was for him to realize how scared she'd been when she thought a snake attacked her.

"Thanks. That was close. It would have been a bit ironic if I'd been killed by the same creature I saved you from."

She realized he still grasped her wrist. She tried to move away, but he pulled her back, obliging her to turn to him.

"You're trembling."

"I'm fine."

"No," he said. "You're not." He pulled her closer

and his eyes softened, his gaze holding her mesmerized. She opened her mouth to try to speak, but in the same instant, he put his hand under her chin and his lips closed over hers.

For a brief moment, she tried to resist but found herself drawn into his kiss as he deepened it, his hand brushing lightly through her hair. For a long moment, time seemed to stand still, and nothing mattered except his lips burning on hers. His tongue teased her own, demanding and insistent, his lips incredibly sensuous, firm, caressing. Through the thin material of her shirt, Cat felt the warmth of his bare chest pressed hard against her breasts. The cold metal of the capsule he obviously did not take off, even to bathe, dug into her skin, but the slight discomfort was nothing compared to the turmoil in her mind.

Without any conscious action on her part, her arms slipped around his neck. She traced the damp skin of his shoulders with her fingers and felt the ridges of old scars on his back. Her heart pounded uncomfortably in her chest, and her blood coursed like liquid fire through her veins.

She couldn't remember ever having been kissed that way, or wanting to kiss someone back so desperately, not even Dorian.

Dorian. The very thought of him quenched the fire in her blood, turning it to ice and driving away the heat of desire, to bring her back to her senses. With that recollection came other memories of the past. Memories of her sister, the reason she'd sworn to kill this man.

Abruptly she broke away. "No, this is crazy."

"Yes," he agreed, his expression once more cold

and dispassionate. "It is—indubitably."

Her senses tormented her with a sudden sense of loss, and for a moment, she wanted to just turn and walk away—confine him to the realms of what might have been. Perhaps he'd thought kissing her would calm her, stop her shaking. If so he'd been mistaken. It elicited quite the opposite effect. She dared to look at him again, at his eyes, once more cool and expressionless.

"A momentary lapse of judgement," he went on. "Any attraction between us is clearly purely physical. Even if things were different, we would probably kill each other in less than a week."

"If we managed to hold out that long," she muttered.

The words were spoken lightly, but despite each having saved the other's life, she knew he still mistrusted her. And nothing had changed her vow to take her revenge on him once she'd made him tell her the truth about what happened to her sister.

****

"We need to get back to camp, or it will be too late to use the antitoxin."

Cat nodded mute agreement. They walked the short distance back to their small encampment in silence.

Kerry gave himself the necessary shots, while she checked the supplies and divided the rations. They sat on the ground and ate their frugal midday meal, keeping a keen watch for unwelcome intruders.

"How much food is left?"

"Enough for a couple of days. We're running low, but that shouldn't be too much of a problem. There seems to be more plant life after the storm. We can supplement our rations with fruit and berries. We're not likely to starve, and Shifter's an omnivore, he'll look after himself." She nodded in the direction of the river. "If we fancy a change of menu, we can always try to catch some fish."

"Maybe, but fishing in the river seems less attractive than it did this morning. Nor do I have any desire to live on fruit and berries and spend the rest of my life on this miserable planet—do you?" Kerry glanced around. "Unfortunately, you seem to have chosen a particularly isolated region on which to crash-land."

"Perhaps that's just as well. We don't know what sort of a reception we're going to get from the inhabitants of any settlements, or if there are any more Union personnel snooping around. Although if there are, I would think they're more likely to make for the more populated areas."

"I would like to know what the Union is doing here in the first place," Kerry said. "Our sensors did not indicate this planet was particularly densely populated or rich in minerals. If they intend landing an invasion force, it hardly seems worth the effort."

"Unless there's more to this world than we're aware of."

"Yes." Kerry fingered the silver capsule around his neck, absently. "Talking of the Union, I suggest now would be as good a time as any to exorcise those ghosts. Is there anything I should know about that officer you were so keen to avoid? Something that might help us both to avoid getting killed?"

She searched his face trying to keep her own expressionless. She'd hoped she would not have to explain about Dorian, but it seemed he was determined to find out. "I'll tell you about him if you tell me about the woman in the locket."

His eyes narrowed. "When did you see that?" he asked, his voice several times colder than the river they both bathed in earlier.

"When you were injured, when we first landed on this planet. I needed to look at it. I thought it might hold a clue to your identity." She'd actually already identified him from her research, of course, but he did not have to know that.

"You no doubt saw the cross as well. That and the locket are priceless—to me." His voice was dangerously soft. "Anyone who tried to steal them would regret it."

"Then it's just as well I didn't stoop so low as to steal from an unconscious man." The pain she saw in his eyes told her it would be wise not to probe more deeply, but somehow she couldn't help herself. "She was very pretty—the woman in the locket."

"She was my mother. I never knew her. She died when I was scarcely more than a baby."

"I'm sorry."

"No need to be. It was a long time ago, as I said. I was too young to remember her. The locket is the only thing I have of hers now."

"The cross wasn't hers too?" He remained silent for so long she wondered if he would ever answer her. This time it seemed she'd pushed too far. "I'm sorry, I shouldn't have asked. It's none of my business."

"No." Another, shorter, pause. "But if it makes you happy, and since we are supposed to be exorcising our ghosts, you might as well know. The cross did not belong to her. It belonged to a woman…a woman I cared for a great deal." He stared at her with the blue gaze that seemed to look into her very soul, and yet somehow straight through her. "Her name was Jestine Darnell—Jess. Before you ask, she is dead too. She died from a laser bolt intended for me. Satisfied?"

The anguish in his eyes, the pain in his voice, almost tore her in two. For the moment, forgetting she'd sworn to kill him, she fought the urge to reach out, to touch him, offer some words of comfort. This man, she found so fascinating, was in love with a phantom from the past, and clearly the hurt ran deep and raw, far deeper than any physical injury he'd sustained over the last couple of days.

"I didn't mean to open old wounds or stir up unhappy memories. Let's just forget this conversation."

He leaned closer. "No, it is your turn. You don't get out of it. Who is that man with the Global Union? He is more than a casual acquaintance, isn't he?"

She drew in a deep breath and nodded. "Yes…it was a long time ago. I've been trying to forget him for over six years." She hesitated. "I was very young and rather naïve, I suppose. I trusted him—and he betrayed me and almost got me killed. Many of my friends lost their lives through him."

"Go on."

"How much do you know about the Union's actions recently?"

"We have been following their activities since we left Earth, eight Terran years ago. Jon and I built the *Destiny* together, to get away from their oppression. It is clear from the internal holo-casts we intercepted that the regime is becoming more and more tyrannical. It spreads itself across the galaxy and swallows up any planet, or group of planets, too small to oppose them, or that refuses to ally with them. All in the name of the *Universal Spirit*, of course."

She gave another nod. "They're not the first regime to use religion as a cover to get the populace to obey them blindly. But not everyone obeys them without question. For years genuine followers of the Universal Spirit have tried to live by and keep alive the true message of their faith while ostensibly carrying out the Union's rulings."

Kerry's face did not change from its impenetrable expression. "I know. Jess was a missionary with the Universal Sisterhood. She was the most genuine, caring person I have ever known, and the bravest." He held her gaze as he asked, "What are your connections with the Sisterhood?"

"None. But as well as the Sisterhood, several other underground movements oppose the Union."

"That is hardly surprising information. So how do you fit into this?"

She tried to keep her voice from faltering. The memories still hurt. "I was one of the Union's officers," she said at length. "I really believed I was working for a great cause, ensuring peace and helping to keep law and order on Earth and the Allied Planets. Then one day they publicly executed a woman for treason. I didn't know her personally, but rumours were rife. I came across evidence that she'd been falsely accused of being a member of one of these groups and, in reality, her only crime was refusing to act as a Union spy. That was when I realized how corrupt the Union was." Cat drew a deep breath before continuing.

"I knew about the underground movements of course, but had no idea how to contact them. Then Dorian Krell, a fellow officer, moved into the apartment next to mine. We saw each other often, and after a while, we became lovers. He let slip he wasn't entirely happy with the way things were going. People executed for the slightest thing, liberties being more and more eroded. He told me he knew the Union used mind drugs on the workers in their factories. Eventually he invited me to join a group he belonged to, working to overthrow the top-level officials and regain the freedoms we'd all lost, as the Union grew stronger and more ruthless."

"A tall order considering how powerful the Union is, and how much of the galaxy it controls."

She nodded a brief agreement. "Yes, but I—we—believed if we could get rid of those at the top, we could band the masses together and start a universal rebellion. There's strength in numbers. The Union is controlled from Earth. If the Central Government could be overthrown, its stranglehold would be broken."

Kerry remained impassive. "So what happened?"

"There was a raid. The Union troops stormed the underground hideout where our group met. Most of the group were killed. I couldn't find Dorian. We had a secret emergency exit via a ventilation shaft, and I led as many of the survivors as I could to safety. Eventually, the troopers discovered the shaft, and in the ensuing fight, I was injured. I found out later, they thought they'd killed me. I hid until they gave up their search, and I could crawl to safety. I thought at the time Dorian had been captured or killed. It was a long while before I discovered he'd betrayed us."

She fell silent for a long time, the pain of the revelation searing her heart. "It's a long story, but one of the other resistance groups found me and the few remaining survivors and took care of me until I recovered. They helped us get away and make contact with a man who forged new identities for us." She felt a rush of anger, recalling how she and the group were betrayed. "Dorian was responsible for the deaths of many of those who had become my friends. I obviously meant nothing to him. He'd just been using me." She chewed on her bottom lip, fighting down her rising anger. "I wish I could've killed him when we saw him yesterday."

"Then why didn't you? You were within range."

She gave him a cool look. "And have the rest of the party on us in seconds? They'd have killed us both. This is my fight, not yours."

"I rather think you have made it mine as well." He paused for several moments. "And about what happened earlier. We both agreed it was a mistake. Even if we were not on a dangerous planet with no contact with my ship, even if there were more than a physical attraction between us, I am bad luck. It looks like we need to work together for the present, but as soon as you get the chance, leave. Get as far away from me as possible."

She stared at him. Did he really believe that, or was this his way of protecting himself from having his heart broken again? "I don't believe in luck, good or bad—and I don't believe you do either."

"I exposed one of our crew members as an agent for the Grakks, which makes me indirectly responsible for her capture and possible execution. Another left the ship because of me, and…" his voice dropped so low his words were barely audible, "the woman I loved threw herself in front of a laser to save my life. I'd call that fairly conclusive."

The bitterness in his tone chilled her blood, but his earlier admission was what jolted her senses, driving away everything except the need for revenge. He'd exposed a woman crew member as an agent for the Grakks and was probably responsible for her capture and possible execution. She'd been right all along. Any last doubt in her mind swept away. This man, for whom a short while earlier she felt such compassion, just admitted the very thing that had, for so long, driven her to seek revenge.

Chapter Nine

In one fluid movement, her weapon appeared in her hand, aimed at Kerry's heart.

She leaned across and scanned his face, expressionless and impassive as always. At the same time, she tried to maintain contact with eyes that threatened to drown her in to their icy depths.

He raised an eyebrow by the merest fraction, almost as if he'd been expecting her to threaten him. As if she were playing some sort of children's game and the weapon she held was a mere toy.

"I thought we decided to call a truce while we exorcised our ghosts."

"That was before you admitted to killing my sister."

His eyes narrowed, glinting like cold steel. "You are either crazy, or lying for some obscure reason of your own. Jess did not have a sister."

"Jess? You can blame yourself for her death, as well, if it makes you feel better, but I was referring to Shalina."

*"Shalina?"* His face hardly flicked a muscle, but she could hardly mistake the shock in his voice. "I knew there was something familiar about you—although I can't say the resemblance is particularly striking for sisters.

"We were half-sisters, to be accurate." She

tightened her grip on the weapon and jerked it meaningfully. If he thought he could distract her and make her drop her guard, he was mistaken.

"And you are accusing me of her murder?" he went on, his voice devoid of all emotion, but cold as the icy heart of a comet. "Don't you know she was transported to the penal colony of Salmar after she failed to capture the *Destiny* for the Grakks? Are you aware she tried to capture our ship and pretended to be in love with Jon as part of her scheme?"

Cat stared at him. Of course, she knew about Shalina's imprisonment on Salmar, the Grakk penal colony. Over the years she'd tried to trace Shalina, she amassed many snippets of information, some of them hearsay, some of them confidential reports she stole or obtained through bribery. The most recent reports, however, all indicated Shalina was tortured to death.

"How *dare* you accuse her of such things? You're the one who's lying. I don't believe you." She glared at him, feeling her face burn, scarcely able to stop herself from lunging at him and activating the trigger.

"Believe me or not. I am not in the habit of telling lies." His eyes gleamed dangerously. "There are very few women I trust, and I knew Shalina was up to something from the beginning. The Grakks' methods are harsh, but she brought it on herself." He leaned a little closer, ignoring the gun. "Although, unless you know something different, it is even possible she could still be alive."

"You don't really believe that do you? And even if she is—as a prisoner of the Grakks? You know as well as I do, she would be better off dead. You might as well have killed her yourself."

She quelled the rage threatening to take away her reason. It would not take much to shoot him now, but if there *was* any chance Shalina still lived, if he knew anything that might help her find her sister, she would make sure he told her before she silenced him for good.

"How do you work that out?" he growled, his voice dangerously soft.

"You were the one who handed her over to the Grakks. You virtually signed her death warrant."

"I am not sure where you obtained your information, but—"

The crackle of static interrupted his words.

"Kerry…Kerry can you hear me?" The voice over the communicator was audible, if distorted, although the holographic image did not appear.

He held her gaze with his own, the question in his eyes needing no words.

She gave him a curt nod. "Be careful what you say, and don't forget I'm watching every move you make." She waved the gun again for emphasis.

"Jon, where the hell are you? Did you get back to the *Destiny?*"

"Yes, but we couldn't contact you…We weren't even sure you were alive."

"What about Zeldra?"

"It was touch and go for a while, but she'll be all right."

"Any chance of getting down here so I can return to the ship?"

"Did you think we'd leave you down there any longer than necessary? For some reason the airlocks sealed themselves, and we weren't able to launch a ferry until now."

"So you are on the surface now?" he asked.

"Berne and I have just made planet fall and are doing a *reccy* of the area. It seemed wise not to set down in exactly the same area where we were attacked, even though the scanners indicated it was clear. Prepare to take down these co-ordinates."

Kerry withdrew a small screen from his belt and gave the instrument a crisp command. He repeated the co-ordinates after Jon, and made a few passes with his fingers. "You are not too far away. There's just one problem."

"What's that?"

She gave him a warning look and brought the weapon closer to his face. He returned her look with one of his own. "It seems the Union is bent on taking over every planet they can lay their hands on, and that probably includes this one. Just watch your backs."

"But we have no actual quarrel with the Union."

"Well, it seems they now regard anyone who does not actively support the regime as a potential enemy. There is a contingent down here at the moment. They've cordoned off—" Before Kerry finished speaking, the communicator crackled again, and the signal became distorted, and faded before relaying a jumble of shots and indistinguishable voices. "Kerry, stay where you are, we're under attack."

A few more crackles and the communicator went dead.

****

Kerry stared at the instrument and muttered something inaudible, before fixing her with an icy stare. "Are you going to shoot me and destroy any chance you may have of escaping this planet, or do we find out

91

what the hell's going on over there?"

Cat slackened her grip on the gun and clenched her fist in frustration. Revenge could wait. At last, the crew of the *Destiny* had made contact. She wasn't about to screw up her only chance of getting away from this wretched planet. She lowered the weapon, and Kerry sprang with the speed of a deadly Andromedan horn snake. He wrenched her weapon away from her, throwing it to one side, and keeping hold of her gun arm, pointed his own gun at her head.

"I gave you my word I would help you off this planet, and I intend to keep it, but if you ever draw a gun on me again, you'd better use it, or so help me, you will wish you had." He pulled her roughly to her feet, still covering her with his blaster.

The way he glared at her, his gaze icy and unwavering, chilled her to the bone, and she struggled to maintain eye contact. What was he thinking? Despite his words a moment ago, his expression implied he might shoot her anyway. Considering she'd just threatened him perhaps she should expect no less.

A long moment passed, and then he relaxed his grip on her arm, and bent to pick up her pistol. "I will keep your gun for now. I don't have time to play games. We've already wasted too much time. We need to find out what's happened to the others."

He gestured with his blaster, forcing her to stay close to him, a little ahead, and set off at a brisk pace. Mindful of the gun pointed in her direction, she struggled with various emotions as several questions raced through her mind. Had Kerry indeed told her the truth? Did her sister really collude with an alien race to steal the *Destiny*? After her initial fury, and having had time to think about it, she was not even sure if she would really have shot Kerry. Killing anyone in cold blood was against her nature, especially this man, who aroused so many conflicting emotions in her.

When they reached the co-ordinates Jon had given Kerry before they lost contact, the area was deserted, and in the distance a cluster of buildings loomed, silhouetted against the silver clouds.

"They're not here." She reached for her pistol before she remembered she no longer had it. The hairs prickled on the back of her neck. Something other than the disappearance of the *Destiny's* crew felt wrong, but she couldn't put her finger on it.

"I can see that." Despite the sarcasm, Kerry's voice carried an edge that bordered on unease.

"You're sure the co-ordinates are correct?"

"I am quite capable of taking down a simple set of co-ordinates. It would seem we are too late. Jon would have got back to me if they had overcome whoever attacked them." Kerry ran a quick sweep of the area. "The ferry is about a klick away, but according to this reading, there is no-one on board." His hand hovered over his blaster as he scrutinized the area. "They must have been taken prisoner, and, we have to assume, by the Union."

The air chilled. Cat shivered, not just from the tone of Kerry's voice, or the sudden cold of the sharp wind stinging her cheeks. A dank mist drifted down from nowhere. She suppressed another shudder. She'd never come across anything like this strange planet. As suddenly as it came down, the mist dissipated again, and she blinked and stared in amazement. The terrain had altered. The plants, tall and spiny, reminded her of the cacti she'd seen on holograms of the western deserts in nineteenth century America on Earth, and the old, Western historical holo-films she'd watched for hours as a child. She rubbed her eyes. Was she seeing things—how could the landscape have changed so much?

She stole a glance at Kerry. He looked back at her, a scowl darkening his dour expression further. Even he seemed different. The black leather he wore was not the same style, and the gun he still threatened her with, a completely different weapon from the blaster he usually carried. She glanced down at her own clothes. A long dark divided riding skirt, a blouse, and a leather vest. Where were the leggings and tunic she'd been wearing when they left her escape craft? And her emergency pack?

"What sort of trick is this?" she demanded. "What's going on?"

"How am I supposed to know?" Kerry said with ill humour, and she deduced he was more worried about the situation than he wanted to admit He held up his scanner and showed her the screen. "I am definitely getting a reading of some form of life close by."

She shot a sideways glance at him. He appeared not to have noticed the changed landscape. How could he not see the same thing she was?

Cat was about to voice her questions when a gunshot rang through the air. Not the whine of a blaster or the electronic hum of a laser, but a real, old-fashioned gunshot. She'd never heard one in real life but she'd heard many on the ancient re-mastered holo-films she'd so loved as a child. She dived behind the nearest boulder and raised her head cautiously. Again, the air seemed to shimmer. The landscape appeared the same as a moment before, but where was Kerry?

"Don't you worry, ma'am, we've got him covered. We won't let him hurt you."

She looked around. Who *was* this strange man, where had he come from, and what was he talking about? Why should she need protecting? She was quite capable of taking care of herself. Another gunshot rang out, immediately answered by several shots to her right. By her left shoulder crouched the man who had just spoken. She barely had chance to notice the star on his vest and archaic clothing, when another round of firing made her duck down behind the boulder again. She glanced at the two men a short distance to her right, both attired like the first one, in the old Western style.

"Are yuh all right, ma'am—he hasn't harmed you any has he?"

"No, no, of course not. What are you talking about?"

The man with a star took careful aim and then ducked down beside her again. "I guess you're a bit confused. It must have been a shock when he robbed the stage and took you prisoner."

"Prisoner?" she said, screwing up her face in confusion. "What stage? What in the cosmos are you talking about? That man didn't take me prisoner, in fact he saved my life when I was injured. Why are you shooting at him?"

"Now don't distress yourself, ma'am," the man said soothingly. "I reckon you must've taken a blow to the head. Yuh obviously don't recall what happened, do yuh?"

"Oh this is crazy," she said in frustration. "I'm not

staying here. I don't know what's going on, but—"

The stranger with the star touched her on the shoulder. "Come on now, little lady, surely yuh remember. See now, it's all coming back to you ain't it?"

She thought back to the events earlier that day. Of course, how could she have forgotten? She'd been on the stage when the outlaws attacked. The man who was shooting at them stole all her valuables and rode off with her. What his intentions were she shuddered to think, but thank goodness the sheriff and his men were on hand to rescue her. She wasn't quite the helpless female the sheriff seemed to think her, though.

"Here, let me get a shot at him," she said, realizing a weapon of her own sat in her holster. She drew the pistol and inspected it more closely. She recognized it as a standard Colt .45. Why should it seem so unfamiliar? She eased back the trigger and aimed at the man in black, but her shot went wild. Darn, she'd missed; she wasn't used to this weapon. How come it didn't seem like the one she normally carried?

An answering shot echoed across the rocks, and the man at her side crumpled with a yell, shot between the eyes. She blinked, the smoke from the gunfire almost making her choke. She could not help but admire the shooting of the man in black, but he wouldn't get chance to let off another shot if she could help it. She took careful aim, and again managed to duck down and avoid the answering fire. She glanced to the side. Both the other men lay stone cold dead. She was on her own against this one then. Why did she have the feeling they were really on the same side? She shook her head, and points of light flashed across her eyes. Her head throbbed. Did she fall from her horse? Had she, in fact, suffered a blow to the head?

*Think. Think clearly, you're in a tight spot and you need to get out of it quick.*

She aimed her pistol for another shot. The man in black was good at avoiding her fire. She'd give him that. But she was a good shot. Her bullets should have reached their target. The man raised his pistol, and she heard a click and ducked down again. It sounded like he was out of ammunition. She risked another look. She could see no sign of him. She heard a rustle in the grass and saw a movement, but he rolled over, avoiding her shot. This one was wilier than a rattlesnake. She aimed again, but he'd disappeared. None of this made sense. How in tarnation could a grown man just disappear in broad daylight? She strained her eyes, trying to see movement where she last spotted him.

A slight noise made her spin round. He was right behind her. He turned and she squeezed the trigger. The weapon failed to fire. In desperation, she holstered it and leapt at him with her bare hands, kicking out at him with all her strength.

\*\*\*\*

Kerry had been in dangerous situations often enough, but this one had him shaking his head in frustration. How had Cat managed to retrieve her weapon? It was in his belt a moment ago. Sheltered behind a neighbouring rock, she seemed to fire wildly, instead of taking aim with the precision he knew she was capable of, and the assailants who opened fire on them appeared to be invisible. He must have killed several of them even so, judging by the screams of pain and a lessening in the intensity of the laser fire. He let loose another blast, and when it did not result in any answering fire, risked a quick look in his opponents' direction. A movement in the rocks caused him to activate the trigger, and he cursed when the weapon did not respond—it should not have run out of charge already.

The next moment, something hit him hard in the back and hands clawed at his face, as he bent his head in defence. It took him a moment to realize Cat clung to his back, apparently trying to gouge his eyes out. He bent over and flipped her neatly onto her back.

She leapt back to her feet in an instant, whirling around and kicking out with her booted foot. He ducked out of her way, and before she could attack again, caught hold of both her hands, then twisted her arm behind her back.

"Stop struggling," he hissed at her. "I am stronger than you are, and I have no particular wish to hurt you, but I will if I have to."

He felt her relax a little and swung her around to face him. She attempted to raise her arm to strike him, and none too gently he forced her to lower it. She stared at him, eyes wide and staring.

"Cat, what the hell is the matter with you? Do you *want* me to kill you? We are supposed to be looking for Jon and Berne, not fighting each other in the middle of the desert. We can settle our differences once we've found them."

She hesitated, and appeared to draw herself back to reality with an effort, shaking her head and blinking.

"Kerry? I-I—what happened?"

"I have no idea," he said, "but at least you seem to have regained your senses, or some of them."

She screwed up her eyes as if trying to see past him, to something beyond. "Something very strange is going on here, though. It's almost as if someone—or something is trying to get us to kill each other."

He did not miss the irony of her words. "Talking of which, I see you have also regained your weapon. I am not sure how you managed it, but is there any chance you will not shoot me in the back the first chance you get?"

"I've told you before, *when* I shoot you, you'll be facing me." Cat removed her gun from its holster and stared at it. "You took this off me, so how...? A moment ago, this was an old fashioned pistol, and out of ammunition." She scanned him up and down as if not believing what she saw. "And you were dressed like an outlaw from the Old West of ancient Terran history, only you were shooting at me from those rocks over there. And my clothes changed too and I didn't have my emergency pack." She patted it as if for reassurance and stared at the buildings in the distance. "That town down there looked like an old fashioned frontier town from the same era."

"I saw nothing like that," he said, drawing his lips into a tight line. "And I was too busy trying to stop myself from being killed by whoever was shooting at me to shoot at *you.*" A suspicion flashed across his mind. "Are you using hallucinators?"

"No, of course not. Do I look like someone stupid enough to let myself end up with a brain turned to mush, like one of the walking dead?"

"I needed to check. One thing is certain, someone was shooting at us, and we have to make sure they're not still alive."

Cat glanced sideways. "I don't understand. There were two bodies here last time I looked. They can't have disappeared."

"You're looking in the wrong place." He nodded toward the area where the firing had come from and strode off glancing over his shoulder to make sure she followed. "You are disorientated—or psychotic."

She glared at him. "No, I'm not. I wasn't hallucinating, or at least I don't think I was. I could smell gun smoke. It was nothing like the emissions from a blaster."

"Perhaps you were under a spell," he said with no attempt to hide his sarcasm. He stopped. They were near the boulders their opponents used as cover in the exchange of a few minutes before. For a moment, the air seemed to shift, and he glanced around beginning to wonder if he was losing his reason himself. There were no bodies, and no evidence of anyone ever being there. Furthermore, the whole terrain seemed to have changed. The ground where they stood dropped off gradually to a wide strip of sandy ground, near a fast-flowing river, bordered by trees and luxuriant shrubs, in complete contrast to the desert landscape they just left. He pushed back a lock of hair from his eyes and stared at her in disbelief.

"This is impossible. Bodies do not just vanish." He took his scanner from his pack and studied it carefully. The data made no sense. Perhaps it too was affected by the solar flares.

Cat took a few steps back as she looked around, handgun at the ready. "Well, they did before, so why be surprised now? Perhaps we are both hallucinating." He looked up from the instrument as she cried out in alarm, the ground around her liquefying as it pulled her down into its depths.

Chapter Ten

"Don't struggle. It's quicksand. The more you try to free yourself the more you will sink."

"I know. I'm not an idiot." Cat took a deep breath and tried not to let panic sweep over her. She held her pistol high above her head, and reached her other arm toward him. "Give me your hand…please."

Kerry shook his head. "That would be a stupid thing to do."

A shock wave ran through her, chilling her blood. "What? You're just going to leave me here?" Perhaps she deserved it. After all, she'd threatened him with a laser-pistol a few hours ago, and just attacked him, albeit while under some kind of hallucination. Would he really let her die in the quicksand? She shuddered at the thought of being left to die slowly in the suffocating wet sand. "Shoot me then, and at least make it quick. Don't let me get sucked under…"

"Don't be so dramatic. If this is typical of most quicksand, you won't sink completely. I'll not risk being pulled in there with you, though." He paused. "Not to mention you could dislocate your shoulder if I tried to pull you out."

"What then?" The sand sucked greedily, and she felt herself sink a little deeper, despite her determination not to make any movement, however slight.

"First, throw me your pack and your handgun before you sink any further—it will help not to have the extra weight. Careful, try not to move too quickly."

She tugged the strap of the pack to release it, and tossed it toward him. She grimaced as she felt herself sink even more. Kerry caught the pack with one hand and she tossed him the gun. He laid both items on the ground to one side.

"Now what?"

"Quicksand is not usually very deep. Can you feel the bottom?"

She pushed down gingerly with her feet. She could feel nothing—absolutely nothing—beneath them. "No, and I'm sinking further." She took another deep breath and tried to keep the panic out of her voice.

"All right. Try and ease yourself forward, so you are lying horizontally on the surface. If this quicksand is like that on most other planets, it's just sand and water. You need to make yourself as buoyant as possible."

"Easy for you to say, standing on solid ground," she retorted. Nevertheless, she succeeded in wriggling her torso and arms enough to push herself forward until her upper body lay flat on the surface, making sure to keep her head up. She didn't want to drown or suffocate in her efforts to escape.

"Good, now try to bring your legs up and lie horizontally on the surface."

It felt as if her legs were made of lead. The sand seemed be almost sentient in its fight to thwart her frantic attempts to pull free.

"*Slowly.* You will just get sucked in further if you try to move too fast."

She drew in her breath, and using all her strength, managed to pull her legs up, one at a time, until she could lie flat on top of the glutinous sand.

"You should be able to 'doggy paddle' your way out now, as if you were swimming."

She stretched out her arms, and inch by inch, succeeded in making slow progress toward him.

"Keep going, you are nearly there."

She felt the ground beneath her solidify and with one last kick, managed to wriggle free as Kerry grabbed both her arms and helped her haul herself clear of the clinging sand.

"Thanks." She sighed with relief, stepping back and resisting the temptation to lean against him, and attempted to regain her composure. The wet sand caked her clothing, weighing her down. Her garments clung to her, and her feet felt like her boots were made of lead. That had been too close for comfort. "I wouldn't have blamed you if you'd left me here," she admitted.

"You probably deserved it, but I am not quite as heartless as you seem to think. Or perhaps I am just getting soft." He nodded at her sand and dirt encrusted clothes. "You need to get those clothes off until they are dry and you can brush the sand off, otherwise it will rub your skin raw."

Cat inclined her head toward the buildings on the other side of the river. "I was thinking we might be able to get rooms for the night in the town over there. We're not likely to be able to find our way back to my escape craft before dark." She put her tri-dee viewer to her eyes and made a sweep along the river. "I can't see a bridge, so it looks like we're going to have to swim if we want to cross to it. I'll keep my clothes on, thank you."

****

Kerry looked toward the structures she indicated. At this distance, with the daylight fading fast, it was not easy to judge, but they appeared to be mostly small, single story buildings. They looked somewhat primitive and reminded him of historical Terran images he'd seen years ago, before he and Jon set off on their explorations in the *Destiny.*

He reached for his blaster and ran his fingers over the familiar bulk of the weapon. He took it from its holster and checked it carefully. It registered full charge again. Something to be to be thankful for, at least.

"Be careful. It seems we can trust nothing, not even what our own eyes tell us." He consulted his chronometer. "It's nearly dusk. If we're going to cross the river, we'd better do it now, while we can still see what we are getting into, and before the sand dries on your skin."

The river turned out to be little more than a stream, not as deep as he initially feared, nor as wide. Holding their packs and firearms over their heads, they were able to wade across the shallowest part. He kept a sharp lookout for any predators like the one that attacked him after he bathed. He glanced behind to see Shifter following, half swimming, half plunging in the shallow water. Once on the other side, Cat placed her pack and pistol on the bank and ducked down under the water to rid herself of any remaining sand. Back on dry land, she shook like a dog and wrung the worst of the moisture from her hair and clothes.

"At least I feel clean again, and it won't take too long to dry off," she said. "The air's still warm, even though it's getting dark."

He surveyed the tall unprepossessing buildings in the distance, squinting through his viewer. "According to our computer, the inhabitants of this planet are technologically advanced, but they seem not to have developed space flight yet, so the chances of them being able to help us leave this planet seem pretty dim. It appears there are automated vehicles moving along the thoroughfares though and there's always the chance they might be able to shed some light on our communication problems."

"I know it was my suggestion," Cat said, "but I'm wondering if coming here might not have been such a good idea after all."

He gave her a withering look. "Why not? No one has seen us up close, so even if the Union personnel are around, we should not be recognized. According to our computer's analysis of the lifeforms on this planet, the most advanced species is humanoid, so we should not look too out of place. We need to find lodgings for the night."

"True, but…" her voice trailed off, and she looked uncertain.

"What's the matter, are you worried about your former boyfriend?"

"Naturally. I would really prefer not to run into him."

"Then we had better make sure we don't."

"What do we do for money?"

"I have no more than a hundred credits. What about you?"

"The same," she said. "So it looks like it'll be just the one room then. Let's hope they accept interstellar currency here."

"And they speak Common Universal." Kerry glanced down at the animal at Cat's side. "We can't take Shifter with us. I know he blends in, but he will be safer here, just in case we run into trouble."

Cat knelt and spoke into the creature's ear and watched as he melted into the undergrowth. "I told him to stay close and that we'd be back."

Kerry raised an eyebrow, as his lips formed a cynical grin. "And he *does* understand everything you say."

She dismissed the sarcasm with a wave of her hand. "He's cleverer than you think. He'll be all right. He'll be able to fend for himself out here."

They reached the small town and wandered around the backstreets, trying to dodge the glare of the streetlamps and look as inconspicuous as possible. Thankfully, the inhabitants were, as he had predicted, to all intents and purposes human, and no-one seemed to take any notice of two strangers in their midst.

They stopped in front of a squat building, the colour of alabaster beneath red and gray streaks and stains of grime and dust. The holographic legend on the wall, written in about a dozen languages, including Common Universal, proclaimed it to be an inn.

He scanned it quickly. "I will go in first. Stay behind me and get ready to make a swift exit at the first hint of danger."

"Yes, *sir*."

He ignored her mocking tone. He doubted she would run if trouble erupted anyway, but no one could say he had not tried to keep her safe.

****

Cat took a seat in the lobby while Kerry went to the reception area to book in. She looked around trying to ascertain at what stage of evolution the inhabitants of this planet might be. The bare, featureless walls on the inside were as unprepossessing as the outside of the building. Plain off-white, with nothing to break up the monotony. The old-fashioned info-screen on one side of the foyer, behind the reception desk, was too far away for her to see or hear anything clearly. She assumed there might be some kind of live local news feature, but could discern nothing to give a clue as to whether or not they might be in any immediate danger.

The innkeeper looked as human as would be expected of an inhabitant of an Earth type planet and kept his head down as he consulted the smaller screen in front of him, so she could not see his features clearly. After what appeared to be a spot of haggling, Kerry gestured to her to follow him down a long, narrow corridor. He stopped at the fifth door and keyed in several numbers and symbols on the touch screen. The door slid open, giving them access to a small room with a divan bed, a chair, a work desk, and not much else, but it had an adjoining washroom. She noted with a certain amount of suspicion, the absence of an information and entertainment screen in the room. It appeared the inn was one of the more "down-market" establishments. Kerry made a brief check of the walls, turning up the worn floor coverings, and checking any movable fittings. Then he took a small scanner from his pack and made a sweep of the room before nodding to her.

"There are no hidden cameras or bugs that I can detect."

"Did you expect there to be?"

"No, but it pays to be careful." He nodded toward the divan. "I assume you will want to take the bed?"

*Please, don't do me any favours.* "You are so gallant," she said, "but as it happens I'll be quite comfortable in the chair. I can sleep anywhere."

"Good, then we'll not have to argue over it."

So, he wasn't going to try to dissuade her. Just as well, she wasn't used to being treated like a lady. She'd had to rely on her own wits too long for that.

"Did you find out anything from the innkeeper?"

"Not much. While I was waiting for the credits to be verified, I took note of the public information broadcast. It seems the arrival of the Union has been well received here. Apparently, there is a conference scheduled with the heads of government, to discuss recruitment and to draw up an agreement whereby the Union will promise its protection in exchange for the planet's allegiance."

"I wonder what they want your crewmates for."

"I wonder that, too." He walked over to the beverage dispenser and requested two coffees. He placed one in front of her on the table, before stating, "There is more. It seems there are further contingents of Union personnel due here, the planet could be swarming with them in a few days. We will need to watch our backs."

She took up residence in the chair, which moulded itself to her body and felt more comfortable than she expected, while Kerry stretched out, fully clothed, on the bed.

He looked relaxed for someone who had yet to figure out how to rescue two of his companions and find a way back to his starship. She studied his face surreptitiously and wondered what went on in his mind. Her own thoughts seethed in a jumble of confused emotions. She'd thought she was tired, but all at once, she seemed to lose the desire for sleep.

"I get the feeling Jon's more of a friend than your commander," she said by way of conversation,

"We've known each other for many years. The *Destiny* is a dream we had since we were children."

"You grew up together?"

"Not exactly. We came from completely different backgrounds, but met at the space academy when my aunt decided I was too much trouble for her to care for any longer."

Cat did not reply for a moment.

"You told me you don't remember your mother. What about your father?" She knew she risked a swift rebuff with her next words but her curiosity overruled any sense of caution. "Was he the one who beat you as a child?"

She felt rather than heard his sharp intake of breath, as he looked at her with haunted eyes. "You ask a lot of questions."

"Perhaps I should be less direct. I'm sorry. I was just…curious."

"No, it was not my father," he said after a brief pause. "I never knew him, nor was I able to find out anything about him, other than he 'met with an accident' before I was born." He ran his hands through his hair and looked at her with suspicion in his eyes. "How did you know?"

She forced herself to keep any trace of pity from her voice. He was not a man to be pitied. "Those scars on your back," she said. "Did you think I hadn't noticed them when you were attacked by that creature at the river? They're obviously old, and I don't believe anyone could have done that to you when you were big enough to fight back."

"I was barely ten years old at the time." He spoke so softly she needed to strain her ears to hear the words. "It was when my aunt, who acted as my guardian, and the man she lived with, Drell Iango, found out I had stolen the locket. It was not the first time they beat me, but it was the worst. The wounds took a long time to heal."

Her feelings of concern gave way to surprise, and not just about the fact he seemed to have lowered his guard enough to recall such personal reminiscences to her of all people. "You stole it? But I thought you said—"

He smiled, without humour. "If you can call taking something that was rightly mine 'stealing,' then yes." She answered the pain in his eyes with questions in her own, not wanting to intrude, but intrigued by his words.

"On one of the rare days they'd left me alone in the apartment I managed to figure out the electronic lock to her private rooms. I was just curious. My aunt never allowed me to enter these rooms, and I wondered if there was something she wanted to keep secret. She said they would be away until late that night, but there was always the possibility they might return early. I knew if they caught me, my punishment would be worse than any they'd meted out before, but I was young, and reckless enough not to care." Again, he paused.

She said nothing, afraid to break his train of

thought, knowing he could lapse once more into icy silence if she interrupted.

"There were several boxes on the table by her bed. The first was unlocked, and merely contained some holodiscs…household bills and a few letters. The largest one was a heavy metal chest, which I knew contained her expensive jewellery." He hesitated again, a faraway look in his eyes, almost as if he'd forgotten Cat was there. "I saw her wearing the stuff often enough. It was all heavy and ostentatious, and of no interest to me. It was the smallest box I found intriguing. Made of silver, as far as I could tell, with engraving and enamel work. It looked very old. It took me a little while to figure out the electronic cipher, but when I did, I knew I had found the real treasure…a small ring, far too tiny to fit my aunt's podgy fingers, and the locket. When I saw the image in the locket, I knew it must be my mother. I seem to have inherited her eyes, and we share the same shaped nose." Something approaching a sigh escaped his lips. "I almost remembered her then."

He clenched his fist, the troubled expression returning to his eyes. "I felt there should have been another image, one of my father, but however closely I inspected it, and although I tried every way possible to produce another holograph, there was only the one. If another ever existed, the crystal had obviously been removed."

"Go on," she urged tentatively, after another long pause.

"I replaced the box in the exact spot where I found it. I hid the locket and ring where I knew they would not be found. They'd belonged to my mother. They were rightfully mine. I had no idea if they were valuable, but to me they were priceless, because they were hers. When my aunt and Iango eventually discovered their loss, they beat me severely, as I knew they would. But they never found my 'treasures'. Shortly afterwards, they disconnected my personal cyber-tutor and sent me away to be educated at the formal State Centre for Education, which is where I met Jon. It was just as well they sent me away, since I made a private vow to find a way to kill the pair of them if they ever tried to beat me again."

He paused for several moments, once more, as if his mind were somewhere else, far away. At length, he broke the silence.

"I've told you my story." His mouth set in a hard line. "More than I have ever told anyone…except Jess…Now why don't you tell me what you're really up to. You said you are a freelancer for the Union, but you also said you'd been part of an underground movement working against them. So…did you switch sides again?"

She should have been prepared for him to want some information from her in return. She could hardly refuse to tell him about her past when he'd shared with her what were obviously painful memories.

She took a deep breath and tried to push her previous determination to kill him, and the reason for it, to the back of her mind. Something about the man made her want to trust him. Could she believe him? If he'd told her the truth about Shalina, it seemed the information she'd pieced together was not as reliable as she thought. Had she misjudged him? While not flinching at killing an enemy, perhaps he was not the murderer she'd imagined, nor capable of deliberately sending someone to certain torture or death.

"Not exactly," she began at last. "After Dorian betrayed us, and I changed my identity, I stowed away on board a ship carrying contraband. They discovered me of course, but if they'd given me up to the Union, they'd have been arrested for smuggling and their ship would've been seized. Besides, most of them had reason to hate the Union themselves. They turned a blind eye, and let me crew with them until we reached a minor planet where I could blend in and get lost. For a while, the Union searched for those of us who escaped, but we were small fry, and they were after the ringleaders of the rebels. I heard they were all eventually hunted down—and executed." She closed her eyes for a moment, wishing she could blot out the memory. "I will never forgive Dorian or forget the way he used me."

She bit her lip, glancing down at her hands before continuing. "After a while, I realized a lot of people were making good money as privateers for the Union. I reasoned that if I was on the inside, I might find a way to do them some damage. I changed my identity again—easy enough when you know who to contact— and altered my appearance a little by letting my hair grow long." She managed to meet Kerry's eyes again. "Not that I was likely to be recognized. I wasn't important enough. Eventually, I gained the trust of those in authority and was allowed to requisition and command my own vessel."

It was difficult to tell if Kerry's expression was one of cynicism or amusement. "So you really are a pirate, despite your protests to the contrary."

She could not repress a twitch of her lips, although she managed to control her expression enough not to allow it to become a smile. "Have it your way. I would actually describe myself as more of a double agent. Just so you know, I never killed anyone when I boarded their ship and only took what valuables I knew the Union would expect. I felt bad doing it and let the crews get away in their escape vessels before handing their ships over to the Global Union." She gave an involuntary sigh of regret as she wondered how many of those crews survived. "I hoped as a privateer I might learn something I could use against the Union."

Her aim had certainly been to infiltrate the Union's defences from the inside and do as much damage as she could, but her prime objective was to find and confront this man who now reclined only a meter or so away from her. She'd been trying to track down the *Destiny* for longer than she cared to think about, using the vast resources of the Union whenever she could. Her intention had been to board the ship with her band of androids. To challenge Kerry Marchant about Shalina before carrying out his execution, even if it meant being killed herself. She never imagined she would find herself and Kerry marooned together on this strange, God-forsaken planet—that was an unforeseen stroke of luck. However, she hadn't anticipated the nagging doubts either, or the way he affected her, the feelings he stirred in her. Feelings that got in the way of her desire for revenge.

"Of course." Kerry gave her a very direct look. "You've still not told me how you lost your ship."

No, she hadn't, and she didn't particularly want to, but since they were being honest…

"I got careless, or to be more accurate, complacent. I didn't think anyone would recognize me after all this time. As I said, it wasn't as if I was a leader of the group or someone who might be important to them. However, one of the officers who led the attack when Dorian betrayed us intercepted one of my holo-cast reports. It seems he remembered my face and diverted a military enforcer to bring me in for interrogation. They chased me into this sector of the galaxy and boarded my ship. Of course I put up a fight but I was hopelessly outnumbered, even with my androids, and I barely escaped with my life."

"And how did you?"

"I used one of the modifications I made to my pistol and fired off a smoke capsule on the main flight deck. In the confusion I managed to get to an escape craft—only I didn't reckon on an electrical storm damaging the power cells and forcing me to crash-land."

"And I'm guessing your real name is not Kincaid?"

Cat hesitated. How much could she trust him? It hardly mattered now. She'd already told him enough to ensure her execution if he was of a mind to turn her over to the Union. However, he'd made his hatred of the regime very clear. She shook her head and gave a half-smile. "No—it's actually O'Brien, but I haven't used that name for a long time."

"I see. And during your machinations as—er—*a privateer*, did you learn anything interesting?"

She hesitated again. Whatever her doubts, surely the rest of the *Destiny's* crew deserved to be aware of the Union's latest schemes and dictates?

"How long is it since you were on Earth and had

any dealings with the Union? A lot has happened in the last three or four Terran years, most of it bad." She glanced at him but his expression remained impassive. "As the Union grows more powerful, it becomes more ruthless and all information from them is doctored to make it seem as if they're a benign regime, intent on uniting the planets. In reality what they're planning is to spread across the universe taking over every new world they come across, and destroying any planet daring to oppose them."

"Is that so?" The information did not seem to surprise Kerry. "We foresaw it happening when we left Earth. It is one of the reasons we wanted to dissociate ourselves with anything to do with the Union. Tell me something new."

"What about this then. For the last three years, private vessels any bigger than hyperspeedster 'A' class have been banned from private ownership. All transporters, cruisers, and freighters are now commandeered by the Union and incorporated into their fleets."

Kerry gave her one of his quizzical looks "Now, that *is* interesting. That information has not filtered its way to us and we have been monitoring their coded messages since we left Earth."

"You should find it more than interesting. Don't you realize the *Destiny* could be in real danger?"

## Chapter Eleven

Kerry lifted a laconic eyebrow. "The *Destiny* is more than capable of defending herself. She is extremely well-armed, but I appreciate your concern." His next words caught her by surprise. "Don't you think it's time we called a truce and decided we are working on the same side, at least until we can get off this planet?"

"Isn't that pretty much what we've been doing?"

He smiled his rare, slow smile, and her heart lurched uncomfortably, a tingling sensation coursing through her body. "Perhaps, when we have not been trying to kill each other."

She took a deep breath trying her best to look unfazed. She would not let him know the effect that smile had on her. "I suppose we have to trust each other, for the present. So I promise I won't draw a gun on you again—unless you make me."

"Good. And since we're being so honest with each other, and just for the record, your sister was captured by the Grakks when she tried to escape in one of the *Destiny's* ferries after I found out about her plan to steal the ship. I have always felt responsible, since it was me who exposed her treachery, but I had no way of knowing, at the time, she would try to make a getaway and fall into their hands."

"You're saying you didn't just hand her over to

them?" Was it possible she'd been blaming him all this time for something he was not guilty of?

"No, I did not. She was fully aware of how the Grakks would deal with her failure to complete her assignment. She played into their hands herself, when she ran away in a stolen escape ferry."

The smile had faded, replaced by his usual impassive countenance. "I suggest we get some rest. We don't know what we are likely to face tomorrow."

"You're right, although personally I don't think I'm going to get much actual sleep after today's events."

"Perhaps you should take the bed, for a few hours anyway. I won't sleep for a while and you will have more chance of resting if you lie down properly. We can change over after a few hours."

His words made sense, although Cat felt unsure whether to accept or not. She really didn't want to owe Kerry any more favours.

"Is something bothering you?" he asked, as she hesitated.

For a moment, she thought she saw a flicker of genuine concern in his eyes. "No, not a thing. All right, I'll take the bed for an hour." As he vacated the divan and made for the chair she'd just left, Cat tossed him a thermal blanket from her pack. "You'll need this. It's not as warm in here as it might be."

She kicked off her boots and slipped beneath the shabby, antiquated quilt. At least it looked clean. She wasn't going to undress, for several reasons. They were in a strange place in dangerous circumstances, and they might have to leave at short notice. Also Kerry had seen her in her undergarments once, when he rescued her from the booby-trapped building. She'd be damned if she'd give him the satisfaction of seeing her half-dressed again.

The windows automatically darkened when they dimmed the overhead illumination, but did not manage to block out the light of the moons completely. She folded her arms behind her head and watched Kerry in the shadows. He sat straight in the chair making no attempt to relax. He placed the blanket over his knees, but she could tell by his stance, he had no intention of sleeping. It crossed her mind to ask him if he wanted to share the bed, but the thought of lying next to this inscrutable man brought an unwanted heat to her face and sent her mind wandering off with thoughts she should never entertain. She frowned and closed her eyes. This was not a casual trip to a pleasure planet, and there was a distinct possibility neither of them would survive the coming day.

\*\*\*\*

Her hiding place was small and cramped. Every bone in her body ached. She could not remember when she last ate. How long had she hidden down here in the bowels of the smugglers' ship? And Dorian—where was he? A face invaded her thoughts, dark eyes mocking. Now she remembered. What a fool she'd been. How could she have ever believed he loved her? She knew one thing for sure. She'd never trust another man again. Never. Love was just a cruel trap and men's hearts were filled with deceit. Nor would she fight for ideals again. Ideals meant nothing. The only thing that mattered was staying alive. Somehow, she'd get away, and when she did, she'd work alone. She would never allow anyone to hurt her again.

All at once, the roar of an explosion drove out all other thoughts, and the walls fell in around her. She couldn't breathe. Something heavy lay on her chest and her legs felt numb. Were they broken? If they were, why did she not feel pain? She tried to cry out, but a thick layer of dust covered her face and mouth. She tried again and this time a cry escaped her lips, and she sat up with a start.

"Quiet, do you want to wake everyone in the building?"

Cat opened her eyes. The darkness, though not complete, was an echo of her nightmare. Panic gripped her. She cried out again, not quite sure if she was still dreaming or in the bombed out building, buried alive. A hand clamped against her mouth, stifling the sound. Gradually she made out the shapes of the sparse furniture in the room, and the shadowy figure of Kerry leaning over her.

"Are you going to be quiet now?"

She nodded dumbly and he removed his hand. She swung her legs over the edge of the bed and her feet touched the reality of the hard floor. She stood a little shakily.

"These walls are thin. Let's hope you didn't wake anyone." Kerry's voice was firm, but no longer held its previous sharp edge. She swayed a little and strong arms took hold of her, as light flooded the room.

"Is that better?" he asked.

The sudden brightness of the room's illumination brought her back to her senses. She took a deep breath of relief. "I'm sorry. I dreamt about—about the explosion again."

"You called out Dorian's name."

She felt herself blush. "He's the last person I want to dream about. I'm not the sort of person who normally has nightmares, or who dreams of old lovers." He still held her very close, and she knew she should pull away. But it felt good. What the hell was the matter with her? How could she feel any attraction to him when she'd promised herself no man would get close to her again? Especially this one, who at times seemed even more ruthless than she was herself, and who aroused such a confusion of feelings in her.

"I'm fine now. I won't let it happen again." She tried to draw away from him, from the comfort of his arms, but his grip did not slacken.

"Are you sure?"

She nodded, without conviction.

He pulled her back toward him and looked deep into her eyes.

Something she saw in those blue depths struck her heart. The pain that never left them went so deep. This man bore scars far worse than the physical one running faintly below his left eye...worse even than the mental scars she harboured herself.

Almost without thinking, she put her hands on each side of his face and pressed her lips to his in a brief kiss, then drew back. For a moment he hesitated, before pulling her close again, so close she gasped. He brushed his thumb along her lips, until she parted them in surrender. A shockwave like electricity ran through her, sending her senses reeling in the ecstasy of the moment. She'd sworn never to let a man betray her again. Every man she'd ever known, even her own father, had let her down, lied to her, and deceived her. Yet at this moment, with this man, every nerve in her body ached with sweet desire.

Kerry's touch aroused a longing in her more intense than any she'd felt before, even in the early days with Dorian. His lips claimed hers, demanding, but at the same time with a tenderness that was almost intoxicating. The ache became a deep-seated need she no longer had any wish to resist. She clung to him, afraid she would be unable to stand if she were to let go.

All at once, he released her. Her knees threatened to give way and she took a deep breath, thankful to have the bed behind her for support. He stood back a short pace, still holding her gaze with his own.

"I'm sorry, I can't do this. We agreed. I have already put you in danger. I cannot—I will not risk getting close to someone and then losing them again."

"I'm quite capable of getting into difficult situations all by myself," she said, trying to keep her voice steady. "And you don't strike me as a man who is afraid to take risks." The pain stabbing in the region of her heart had nothing to do with her recent injuries. At least she was capable of thinking straight again. The euphoria, which threatened to overcome her and rob her of her ability to rationalize, dissipated as fast as it came. Her body still trembled despite her efforts to control it, replaced by a vague self-disgust that she could have these kind of feelings for the man she'd once sworn to kill. "Don't worry. I realize that kiss was just a momentary weakness, a diversion to calm my nerves." *Yes a diversion, a bit like keeping a beautiful but very poisonous reptile as a pet.* "I'm not going to ask anything more of you, and we can just forget it ever happened."

"Good, then at least we understand each other. Will you be able to sleep without nightmares now?"

"Don't worry about me. I told you, I'm fine." She managed a feeble smile to cover her show of weakness. "That's the second time I've had a nightmare about the explosion. It's not doing my reputation as a freebooter much good is it?"

"No," he agreed without humour, his face betraying no sign of emotion. He reached out and ran his fingers lightly through her hair again. "And I'll not deny kissing you felt good, but it should not have happened. I told you before, I am bad luck."

"So you said, but I told you I don't believe in luck, good or bad." She sighed. "You take the bed. I want to sit up for a while."

"As you wish," he said, and moments later plunged the room back into darkness.

****

Cat stirred and shifted in the chair. She'd slept a little, after all. The light struggling to filter through the dusty window proclaimed the coming of the dawn and roused her to wakefulness. She checked the time and threw off the thermal blanket. Kerry stood by the window, and as she rose from her seat, he turned to look at her.

"It's nearly morning. Why didn't you wake me?" she asked, keeping her tone casual but realizing it sounded like an accusation.

"There was no point in disturbing you yet. You looked like you needed to sleep."

"And what about you?"

"I had enough sleep. Besides, someone needed to stay alert."

She was about to come back with a defensive reply when she realized his mouth was turned up in that devastating smile. Damn him. He was laughing at her— and why should it bother her so much?

Before she could reply the smile vanished, and he held up a hand. "Listen."

"What?"

Kerry touched the window and stood to the side as it slid open. "I think it is time to get out of here—fast."

She'd already slung her pack over her shoulder and put on her boots. The murmur of voices drifted through the open window from the street below.

"What's up?"

"Take a look, but make sure you're not seen."

Keeping well to the side, as Kerry indicated, she peered past him. A small group, indistinct in the half-light, but clearly in the uniform of the Union, congregated below them in front of the building.

"How do we get out of here?" she asked. "We're trapped."

"Maybe not. We don't know for sure they are after *us*. They have no reason to be—unless your ex-boyfriend somehow found out you are here in this building. Not likely but, nevertheless, it would be wise not to take any chances." He made for the washroom, with Cat following close behind.

"Lucky this window faces the back of the building," Kerry said, keeping his voice low. "There's no one around, come on." He slid open the window and eased his frame through and onto the ledge outside. He held out his hand and she took hold of it, and followed him, trying to ignore the burning pinpricks of electricity that shot through her body at his touch.

Kerry leapt from the ledge to the flat roof of an outhouse adjacent to the inn. He turned and watched as she followed suit. He knelt and delved into his pack. After a moment, he brought out a small coil of synthetic rope and looked around, obviously searching for something to secure it to. A small communications booster jutted out to his left. Kerry threw the end of the rope and it hooked around the small protuberance. He threw the other end to the ground, and to Cat's surprise, it not only reached the ground, but also became rigid once it touched the earth below.

"Come on," Kerry said with some urgency, as he began the descent, hand over hand. She needed no encouragement to follow, and in a few minutes, they were both on the ground. A quick flick of his hand and the rope disengaged itself from the booster to coil itself neatly into a small package that Kerry returned to his pack.

"Walk casually," he whispered, "we don't want to attract attention if we can avoid it." They walked down a narrow alleyway and came out to the main street again.

She paused for a split second to send out an ultra-sonic signal to Shifter. Wherever he was, he should hear it and come to find her. "Do you really think they were after us?"

"No telling. However, I would prefer not to be around any of the Union if I can avoid it. Somehow, though, we still have to find out what's happened to Jon and Berne and where they've taken them."

"And how do you propose we do that?" she asked.

"At the moment I have no idea. Shhh."

Before she could protest, he pulled her into a

doorway and bent his head as if to kiss her.

"Play along," he whispered in her ear. She could hardly call it a difficult feat. She put her arms around his neck, her heart thudding as he pressed his face close to hers. She tried to breathe normally, and hoped he would think it just a reaction to the danger they faced. After a moment, he drew away, the swift movement dislodging her grip on him and almost causing her to stumble backward.

"It's all right, they've gone."

"I assume by 'they' you mean more of the Union?" she said, wishing she could calm the thumping of her heart and hoping she didn't sound as breathless as she felt.

"Yes, there were a couple of them in the street. They have moved on now."

"Thought you didn't want to make a habit of this," she said, but he was already heading off down the road and didn't hear her.

"How are we going to find out where your friends are?" she asked as she caught him up. "They could have been taken anywhere. They might not even still be on this planet."

"That is a risk we will have to take, but my guess is they were taken for a reason, otherwise there would be little point in keeping them alive." He set his mouth in a grim line. "Assuming, of course, they *are* still alive. We have to work on the assumption that is the case. If they are being held captive, with a view to being taken off-world, it's my guess they are probably on that flashy Union cruiser."

"Great. So all we have to do is break into a Global Union starship to rescue them."

They passed through the small town keeping a wary lookout for any more Union officials but they reached the outskirts without any further incident.

"Are we going to stay around here in case we can pick up some clues?" Cat asked as they stopped for a moment to rest.

"No, it's too dangerous. We need to get away, and some transport would be good." He turned back to her, and jerked his head in the direction of an area on their right, adjoining what appeared to be a narrow highway. "There are about a dozen overland hover-cars parked in the bay over there, it should not be too difficult to access entry to one of them."

"You mean steal one?"

"Do you have a better idea?"

"No. It would certainly be nice not to have to walk any further," she agreed.

"Then you had better hope we don't get caught." They retraced their steps to the small vehicle lot, which held an array of hover-cars of various shapes and sizes. He passed two or three before stopping at a shabby, streamlined hover-car in a nondescript silvery gray. "This one will do. It looks small and manoeuvrable, without being too noticeable."

"You want me to 'pick the lock' for lack of a better term?"

"One of your talents?" Did she actually detect a slight hint of admiration in his voice?

"Go ahead," he told her. "I'll keep watch in case anyone comes."

She studied the access panel. It didn't look very different from most of the ones she'd managed to break into before. Drawing a small instrument from her pack, she passed it across the metal. She ran her fingers over a sequence of hieroglyphs on the panel and the side of the vehicle slid back.

"Quick, jump in before someone sees us." She slid into the passenger seat at the front so Kerry could seat himself in the pilot's seat. "I'm not familiar with the controls on this type of vehicle, are you?"

"I have never seen anything remotely similar," Kerry said, studying the control panel intently for a moment. He touched a control and the craft lifted smoothly off the ground. Another control slid the transparent dome over them. A few loud yells followed them as they lifted into the air, and gained height and speed, while the air around them crackled and sparked with exploding energy bolts.

Chapter Twelve

Kerry steered the craft even higher, although it was probably designed to hover no more than ten meters or so above the ground, and increased its speed. "Hold tight," he yelled above the whine of the engine. "I don't want to risk taking a hit from a lucky shot."

Cat clicked her security harness in place and sank deeper in her seat. Kerry manoeuvred the small craft in a series of skilful loops and zigzags that made her stomach lurch, until eventually they levelled out.

"It looks like we lost them. Do you see anyone following us?"

She looked down at the small rear-view scanner in the control panel. "No. I think you're right. There's no sign of any pursuit vehicles."

Kerry made the hover-car swoop in a graceful arc and after some calculations and verbal reprogramming to the on-board nav-system, headed southwest, in the direction of the shallow valley where Cat had crashed her vehicle. "Can you see any form of audio communication panel?"

"Yes, it's right here." She ran her fingers over the controls but the only response was a load of static. "It's either off frequency or scrambled. Hold on." After some adjustments the static resolved itself into a sequence of intelligible broadcasts, in a language she did not understand, and which seemed just as unfamiliar to Kerry. "This is a pretty old vehicle by the looks of it, but there must be a translator." She fumbled with another small control. "Ah, here we are."

The newscast did not tell them much they had not already surmised. The delegation sent by the Global Union of Earth and Allied Planets to Robigo purported to be discussing recruitment and trade. No mention of any prisoners taken and nothing that would help them track down the two missing *Destiny* crewmen.

After several minutes, the broadcast gave way to a jangle of instrumentation, so off key and nerve shattering, she switched it off in disgust. "If that's what passes for music on this planet I'm not surprised they're not more technologically advanced. It's amazing they've got this far."

They travelled on in silence. At length, with a glance at the instrumentation, Kerry cut the speed and reduced their altitude. "We're less than half a klick from the Union ship now. I'm going to head for those trees on our port side and hide the craft there. I don't want to risk it being spotted by any Union lookouts."

"Of course we still don't actually know it's the Union who captured your friends," she said, pursing her lips.

"No, we don't. On the other hand, it is pretty safe to assume it is."

"You've tried contacting them of course, just in case?"

"Of course." Kerry glanced across at her. "However, you don't really think their captors would have allowed them to keep their communicators do you?" he asked in withering tones.

"No—but you obviously thought it was worth a

try."

"Touché."

When they reached the wooded area, Kerry brought the small craft down as close to the trees as feasible, and drove the vehicle under some low branches. As soon as the dome slid open, he jumped out and lay on his back on the ground, to run his fingers over the underside of the hull.

"Now let's see if we can find the tracking device on this thing."

"You think there is one?" she asked.

"I don't intend to take any chances. It may be an old craft, but it seems pretty well equipped and its owner probably doesn't want to lose it. I have no intention of making it easy for them to take it back, not yet anyway, we might need it again."

"You're right. But any tracking device is probably embedded in the computer system. It's not going to be easy to find, is it?"

"Not easy, but not impossible." While she kept a wary watch for any pursuit vehicle, Kerry slid open a small panel and with a few deft movements tapped into the system. After a few minutes, he looked up. "I've found it, but it is linked to a self-destruct system. Deactivating it without blowing ourselves up could be a little tricky."

"So can you do it?"

"Let's say it is not the first system of its kind I have had to deactivate. I should be able to work it out."

She nodded. "Good. Best get a move on then, I imagine the rightful owner of this vehicle will be on our trail sooner rather than later."

Kerry looked at her over his shoulder. "Would you

prefer me to hurry and blow the pair of us sky high?"

She pursed her lips and said nothing. He seemed to know what he was doing. In fact, she knew a thing or two about explosives herself, although she'd not told him as much. She stood by the vehicle and kept watch, expecting at any moment to see a pursuit vessel skim over the trees toward them.

She again made discreet use of her ultra-sonic signaller. Where was Shifter? The creature should have caught up with them by now. The sound was inaudible to humans and unbearable to most animals, but Shifter usually responded to it like a pet dog.

After what seemed like an eternity, Kerry stood and pushed back the stray lock of hair that flopped over his forehead. "That should do it. I've re-programmed the signal to appear to be emanating from a point sixty klicks to the northeast, the opposite direction to our current position."

As he spoke, his communicator crackled and a slightly distorted female voice came across, accompanied by a small holographic image that flickered briefly before stabilizing.

"Kerry…Kerry do you copy?"

"Zeldra, thank the stars we have contact again. Where the hell have you been?"

"It's good to hear you too. We've been trying to contact you."

"And I you. Presumably the problem was sunspots again—or atmospherics."

"Yes, but strangely the computers weren't registering your life signs either. We were getting worried. Are Berne and Jon with you? We've lost contact with them as well."

"No. I'm afraid there is a possibility they have been captured. We're trying to track their whereabouts now. I will let you know as soon as we have anything conclusive." He paused.

"Don't worry. If they have been taken prisoner, it is unlikely they will have been harmed. Their captors could have killed them straight away if that was the intention, rather than take them prisoners. I will try to get back in contact as soon as we have any news."

There was a long pause, and when Zeldra's voice came back, it sounded strained. "I'll keep the channel open. Please find them—and be careful."

Kerry cut the connection and turned back to her. "We've lost enough time. We need to check out that Union ship. It will be dark soon."

"Of course you realize the place could be crawling with Union personnel by now? If anyone's going to kill you, I want it to be me." She kept her tone light, but he threw her a look that would have chilled her to the core if she hadn't come to realize much of his dour attitude was a front.

"We have to find out if Jon and Berne are on board or not."

She nodded. "I know. Zeldra sounded worried when you told her the two crew members of your ship had been captured."

"She is Berne's wife. They have been together for a long time now. It would break her heart if anything happened to him." He stated this in such a matter of fact tone, without expression, she couldn't help giving him an enquiring look. It sounded almost as if he didn't care, but then she saw a flicker of emotion in his eyes and realized how much this man kept hidden.

"They are both medics," he went on. "And very valuable crew members."

She walked beside him through the scrawny trees. Would anyone ever be able to break through the shield he'd built around himself? Would he ever allow himself to care again? And why should it matter to her anyway?

\*\*\*\*

"Do you not think"—Kerry said, as they jogged the short distance to the Union ship and Cat's escape vessel—"this was all a little too easy?"

Cat looked at him with a little crease wrinkling her brow, which he knew meant he had taken her by surprise. "Easy?"

"Yes. Think about it. Disabling the self-destruct on that tracking device was a lot simpler than I anticipated. And we escaped from the inn, stole a hover-car, and although we were shot at, we got away without a scratch."

"You mean you'd have preferred it if we'd been captured—or killed?"

He flashed a look. "That is not what I'm saying. I am just surprised we got away quite so easily that's all."

"Hmm. You may have a point, but it doesn't make any sense—"

He was silent for a moment. "We can't allow ourselves to take anything for granted. We need to stay alert at all times."

Cat was right. It did not make sense. It almost seemed as if someone was playing them, and he'd be damned if he'd stand by and just let it happen.

It took them only a few minutes to climb the dunes and reach the rim of the declivity. The area seemed deserted, but now another vehicle stood next to the ship. A Union transit ferry.

"The broadcast I saw at the inn said there would be several contingents of Union personnel arriving," he said, lowering his voice to a whisper.

They stayed, hunkered down at the top of the incline, weapons drawn. No guards or Union personnel were in evidence. A quick scan did not indicate any lifeforms, although with the problems he'd had communicating with his ship, he should hardly be surprised. After waiting for several minutes, they crept forward a little way down the slope. He waved his blaster toward Cat to indicate she should move across in the opposite direction and check out the area from that side. After a few minutes, she returned to where he crouched with his blaster still at the ready.

"There's no sign of anyone. I can't believe they haven't left any guards."

"They were obviously not expecting anyone to come along and steal their ship—or the ferry. Besides, I would imagine both crafts have a force field around them, like your escape vehicle." He picked up a small pebble lying on the ground and threw it toward the hyperspeedster. It elicited a hiss and crackle, before falling to the ground in a flurry of sparks. "Thought so." He frowned and swore under his breath. "That means I can't scan the ship to find out if there is anyone inside. I wonder how long it would take to disable."

He nodded to her over his shoulder. "Come on, we need to be careful. We will be sitting targets if any of the Union officers or their men are on board and spot us, but I want a closer look."

They threw themselves down on their stomachs

and inched their way forward with some caution. At this point he had no idea what he would do if they were fired upon, other than hope they were not hopelessly outnumbered, but somehow he had to find out if the others were held on this ship.

"She's a beauty, though, isn't she," Cat murmured, her voice hushed to an admiring undertone. "What I wouldn't give to have a ship like her."

The craft rested like a graceful bird sitting in repose on the dusty surface—larger than a standard hyperspeedster, but still small enough to land on a planet. Streamlined and sleek, it also boasted an unsubtle and deadly-looking weapons array. "She's not like the purely serviceable monstrosities the Union normally has in service. I wonder why this one's so different."

"I was wondering that myself," he said. "It could be a prototype. She looks as if she has a lot of refinements most of the Union ships don't have." He paused a short distance away from the ship. "Perhaps the personnel who crew it hold positions of particular importance in the Union hierarchy. There don't seem to be any registration numbers or symbols, which is highly irregular. Now we can see her at close range, I doubt it is a Union design, more likely it has been 'requisitioned', if what you said is correct."

He shot her a sardonic look, then raised his blaster and glanced around. It could be Shifter, the animal came and went like a shadow, but he thought he heard a slight sound behind him.

He looked over his shoulder then peered at the scrubby bushes to the side of him. Nothing. Hell, he was getting jumpy. Nevertheless, he kept his hand on the reassuring bulk of his blaster.

He turned back to check the ship again, and felt the hard muzzle of a weapon between his shoulder blades.

Chapter Thirteen

"Get up, both of you, and turn around, very slowly, putting your weapons on the ground. Don't try anything. I'd be only too pleased to shoot you and leave your bodies to rot."

He recognized that voice—a voice from the past—and from the gasp Cat gave from just behind him, so did she. A thousand questions crowded his mind as he rose and turned to face the woman who held him at gunpoint. She stood motionless, a sneer on her beautifully formed lips. Tall and striking, her wavy ebony hair, now cut short, would have given her a rather masculine appearance if her face were not so delicately sculpted. There was nothing delicate about her expression though. Her eyes glinted, dark gray, like granite, and as hard.

*Apparently, lighting did strike twice.*

The woman before him was the last person he ever expected to see alive.

*Shalina Montalban.* For a moment, he stood stunned, unable to believe the evidence before his eyes.

A glance to the side registered Cat facing a man in Union uniform, who had a blaster directed at her head. She wore a dazed expression as if she too could not believe what she saw. Seeing Shalina must have been an even greater shock for her than for him. He cursed as he laid his blaster on the ground near his feet. He should have trusted his instincts. How could the two people confronting them have sneaked up behind them without a sound? They almost seemed to have materialized out of thin air. The few stunted bushes struggling for survival in the sandy ground were not sufficient to hide behind and there was no other cover in the immediate vicinity. He strained his eyes to look beyond Shalina, half expecting several more Union personnel to appear out of nowhere.

"Kerry Marchant. It's been a long, long time. I've been tracking you and the *Destiny*, hoping I'd catch up with you again and here you are in the last place I expected to find you." Shalina nodded in Cat's direction. "And with Catrina of all people. Rather ironic to see the two of you together."

He ignored the innuendo in her voice. She could draw whatever conclusions about their relationship she wanted. Despite the danger facing him, he could not repress his curiosity. "So you managed to escape the Grakks."

"Yes, I'm sure you believed I was dead, or brainwashed, and no more than a mindless slave by now. I'm sorry to disappoint you. You forget. I'm a survivor. I do whatever is necessary to stay alive. True, I was sent to Salmar and tortured. Not a pleasant planet, Salmar, but the Salmarans are, let us say, interesting. I persuaded my torturer there were…more pleasant ways of spending his time." She flashed him a look of pure hatred. "If it satisfies you, I suffered—a lot. But as I said, I'm a survivor. My torturer eventually turned me over to a Salmaran slave trader, and from there I was purchased by a Union Officer."

"So how *did* you escape?" he asked with cold

curiosity.

She smiled, although the way her lips curled it came across as more of a sinister, self-satisfied smirk. "I made myself so useful to him he gave me my freedom and helped me get a position in the Union. Not long afterward he met with what you might call an 'unfortunate accident,' and I took over the situation he left by his unfortunate demise."

If she expected him to show any signs of admiration, she would be disappointed. The only emotion she evoked in him was one of contempt. She might have evaded the worst of the Salmarans' torture and mind manipulation, but there appeared little humanity left beneath the alluring exterior.

The man threatening Cat stepped closer to her and grabbed hold of her hair with one hand so she could not turn her head away. "Quit the conversation, Shalina. I need to have a word with your sister. If you recall, she has something I want."

He drew in a sharp breath. Cat had told the truth then, not that in his heart he'd ever doubted it. She and Shalina really were sisters. They were of a similar height and build, and their faces showed a slight family resemblance, which explained why Cat looked vaguely familiar when he first saw her. Shalina appeared to be several years older though, and with her hair being jet black and short, the similarities between the two were not immediately obvious.

Again, a sneer crossed Shalina's otherwise almost perfect features. "Plenty of time for that, Dorian. You can have her soon enough. First, let's see how important they are to their crewmembers."

Dorian? So this was the man Cat had been involved

with. What did he want with her now? Pushing the question to the back of his mind, he directed his attention to Shalina. "You want to hold us to ransom? That's crazy. The *Destiny* is an exploratory craft. She does not carry rich cargo or goods…" his voice trailed off as he realized there was only one thing this woman wanted, and he knew the lengths to which she would go to get it.

"Exactly. The ship itself is far more valuable than any cargo it might carry. I failed to get her the first time. This time I won't fail. The Union will reward us with a small fortune, as well as prominent positions in the Supreme Council for bringing about her capture. Now we have both you *and* the commander, I doubt the rest of the crew will put up much of a fight."

"You are delusional," he said. "Do you really think either Jon or myself, or any of the crew would allow you to take the *Destiny*? We would see her destroyed and us with her, rather than let you, of all people, take possession of her."

Shalina laughed, a sound without mirth, and he quelled the sudden urge to lunge at her, to put his hands around her throat and silence her forever.

A cry, which almost sounded like a sob, from Cat made him half turn in her direction. Her face, drained of all colour, contorted in an expression of utter disbelief. For a moment, he met her eyes. A spark of anger shone silver then faded to register a sorrow that twisted his gut, knowing there was nothing he could do to ease her pain.

"Shaz," Cat said, her voice husky with emotion. "What's happened to you? You can't seriously—"

"Be quiet," Shalina almost spat out. "And don't

call me that. I haven't been known by that nickname since—"

"Since you and I were children," Cat finished for her.

"Indeed, dear sister. About as long as the last time we saw each other. Did you ever realize how much I despised you? How tired I was of hearing our mother always praising you and extolling your virtues...the way she doted on you when your father deserted us? Why do you think I left as soon as I could afford transportation off-world? I was sick of being treated as a hanger-on."

Cat stared at her. "It wasn't like that, Shalina. She loved you as much as she did me. So did I. When my father disappeared, she—"

"Be quiet. We don't have all day to stand here, reminiscing. Move," Shalina commanded, and Dorian Krell waved his weapon at Kerry.

Before he could respond a small tree to his left appeared to dissolve, shimmering and changing shape, as a large form leapt toward Cat.

"Shifter," she cried out. In the same instant, her captor looked away from her to stare at the animal. Cat spun round and grabbing hold of his arm kicked out and disarmed him. Kerry took advantage of Shalina's momentary distraction to wrest her blaster from her and pick up his own from the ground.

"Kerry, look out!"

He dodged to one side and whirled round to see Cat fire a rapid salvo into the area behind him, and two men fall forward, to lie motionless.

"Thanks," he said, giving her a curt nod. "Let's hope there aren't any more."

Shalina backed away and spoke urgently into her wrist communicator. "There's a problem here. We need reinforcements—and we need them *now*."

Kerry cast a glance in Cat's direction. She touched a control on her weapon and immediately a cloud of black, choking smoke enveloped the area. "Quick" he hissed in her ear, "Back to the hover-car."

He grabbed her arm and they dived into the scrub, speeding back up the slope along the tree line, using the slender trunks as cover. They bent low and raced across the dunes, along the sandy landscape and through the trees, to where their stolen transport lay hidden. They barely made it back to the vehicle, gasping and choking for breath. As they scrambled on board, a volley of blaster fire caused the air to shift and the vegetation around them to shrivel and turn brown.

"The reinforcements wasted no time arriving. Let's get out of here." His fingers sped across the control panel, and he used all his skill to utilize every atom of power the vehicle possessed. He guided it out of the trees, oblivious to the branches snapping, as he backed out beneath the low boughs and coaxed it above the ground.

The atmosphere exploded in clouds of electrical energy as blaster fire once more rained all around them. His mind teemed with questions in need of answers, but now was not the time to ask them. The little vessel was not easy to control, especially when fired at from several different directions.

He fought to keep the vehicle steady, as it pitched and rolled, despite his efforts to keep it hovering on an even course.

He glanced at Cat. She'd wedged her gun in the

gap between the body of the craft and its partially closed dome, so she could fire on the Union personnel below, but a single weapon was not going to hold off their adversaries.

A curse escaped his lips, and his knuckles clenched white on the controls. If only this thing had more speed. They needed to put greater distance between themselves and the Union. There were laser bolts as well as blaster fire. If one hit the vessel…The thought no sooner entered his mind than a small explosion to the rear sent a shudder through the craft and the controls went dead as the craft plummeted toward the ground. *So much for things being too easy*. It seemed their luck had finally run out.

He struggled to regain control of the hover-car but nothing responded. The engine screamed and black smoke enveloped them, bringing with it an acrid, sulphurous stench. Flames licked across the control panel and he tried to smother them with one hand, while attempting to regain control of the craft with the other. It took all his willpower to concentrate on the craft and ignore the excruciating pain that ran up his arm and spread across his body.

The trees and brush sped up to meet them. He wrestled in vain with the now useless controls and shouted to Cat to stop firing and brace herself for the inevitable impact with the ground. Seconds later, they ploughed into the earth and came to a shuddering stop. Then blackness enveloped him like a shroud.

Chapter Fourteen

*Apparently, lighting did strike twice.*

The woman before him was the last person he'd ever expected to see alive. For a moment he stood, stunned, unable to believe the evidence of his eyes. His hand felt as if it were on fire. He stopped himself looking at it with an effort and aimed his blaster, staring across the space dividing him and the woman. *Shalina.* Shalina Montalban as he'd known her on the *Destiny.* He'd always suspected her given name was a fake.

A strange feeling of *déjà vu* came over him, as if he had been in this situation before. What in the name of the *Universal Spirit* were they doing back here, when they could have been better occupied working out a strategy to rescue his shipmates?

Shalina glared back at him, her blaster drawn, as were those of the half dozen or so men ranged around her. He looked across at Cat, whose finger also hovered over her trigger.

He tried to focus. He must be tired, or perhaps it was the pain. His vision appeared to be getting hazy. The figures before him blurred and shifted, like a poorly transmitted holo-cast. All at once, the scenery changed. Gone were the trees, the rocks, the drab landscape, and the smoking wreckage of the hover-car. They now stood in a tall, high ceilinged room. What was going on? Was this another thaumaturgy or illusion? Was Cat experiencing the same thing?

Large, hexagonal windows let in the light, but he could see nothing through them. The impression was like looking through layers of opaque material, gossamer thin, but blocking out all but that unearthly, glowing, light. Unlike any natural sunlight, it rolled against the windows resembling the shadows of waves upon an alien sea, and he could not shake off the feeling it was as much an illusion as the room itself.

Ranged around the room were several high-backed benches occupied by stern-faced figures, wearing scarlet, hooded robes. A long, low table in front of him dominated the room. In the centre, sat a single, ostensibly female figure also robed and hooded, but whose garment shimmered iridescent silver, flanked on either side by figures in robes of white. Both she and the other figures were very tall and gaunt, and clearly not human. Their skin reflected an almost metallic pearl gray. From beneath the hoods that hid most of their face, wisps of hair shone like drifts of winter snow, but whether from age, or as a natural characteristic of their species, he could not tell.

He stole another glance at Cat, who stood to his right, rock still, as if mesmerized, her face registering shock and disbelief. He raised his weapon and aimed it at the figures before him. They appeared unarmed. *Let's see how they react to a threat.*

"There is little point in firing your weapon. You will find it is inoperative."

He fired at a point on the far wall behind the speaker. Nothing happened.

"I told you your weapon was useless. Why do you humans not believe what you hear?"

"What do you want with us?" he asked, keeping his voice calm and controlled with an effort. For the moment, at least, it seemed best not to antagonize their captors. "Who are you and why have you brought us here?"

Shalina, Dorian, and the others in the Union contingent stood lined up next to him on his left. Cat, on his right, took a small step sideways toward him. It struck him that, standing as they were, the situation resembled being in the dock of an old fashioned Terran Courtroom. Looking past Cat, he registered, to his amazement, the presence of, not only, Jon and Berne standing next to her, but the telepath, Regin, together with Zeldra. That meant the whole crew, apart from Delian who must still be on board the *Destiny,* were now prisoners. He cursed under his breath. Could things get any worse? At least Jon and Berne were alive, and Delian appeared to have avoided capture.

"Order!" The figure in the silver robes said loudly. "You are not here to engage in conversation with us. You will speak only when addressed directly. As for your question, you are all on trial. Since you feel the need to identify us, you may refer to us as 'the Therocians'. You have trespassed on this planet and engaged in fighting among yourselves with no thought as to the consequences, despite attempts to deter you."

"Permission to speak," he asked, trying to keep his tone civil, despite his growing anger.

She shot him an icy stare. Shafts of light appeared to emanate from her eyes. "You will be given a chance to speak in due course, human. Since you have the temerity to trespass on this planet without authority or permission, you will stand trial before this tribunal, for your crimes and those of your species."

Cat turned her head a fraction toward him, her expression mirroring his own mystification.

"These crimes are manifold," the entity continued. "You kill your own kind. You have little regard for the survival of your own planet. You have annihilated whole species of animals that shared it, polluted your seas, and killed the aquatic life. You caused such destruction to her climate and atmosphere with your greed and lust for comfort and luxury, your species is now obliged to live under domes with artificial life support systems. Furthermore, you have spread yourselves across the galaxy and inflicted your ways and customs on the rightful inhabitants of these planets to the detriment of their established values and way of life, and taken possession of their home worlds. The human race is like a deadly virus spreading across the universe to infect everything it touches."

She paused and stared at the group. "These are the crimes with which you are charged. What do you have to say for yourselves?"

"You can't charge a small group of people with the wrongs of the whole of humanity," Jon said, echoing his own thoughts. "These have been perpetrated over many centuries. The destruction of Earth's climate and atmosphere began several centuries before any of us were born. Not all who call themselves human are murderers and destroyers of the natural life of our Earth."

"That is acknowledged, and this was taken into account when your trials were set."

"Trials?"

"Yes." The figure before them on the left now

spoke. "From the moment you landed on this world, we set you a series of assessments to see how you would react. It is incomprehensible to us why members of the same species, who call themselves advanced, should seek to slaughter each other. So we decided to see how you would react when forced to face danger together."

The silver-robed being who spoke first inclined her head toward Cat. "You had a choice," she said. "You could have left this man, whom you seem to regard as your enemy, to his fate, but you chose instead to tend to him, regardless of your own safety. This surprised us so we decided to set another task to see what the man you saved would do when faced with a perilous situation." She turned her attention back to Kerry.

"You too passed the trial we set you. It would have been easy enough to leave the woman to die beneath the rubble of a ruined building. You could not guarantee either that the danger was past, or after saving her she would not die from her injuries. Nevertheless, you took it upon yourself to remove her from the danger and to tend to her, even though neither of you trusted the other. We did not expect to find this facet of compassion in humanity. Our observations have shown greed and self-preservation to be the prevailing instincts of your species. This is our first opportunity for first hand observation. We have found it an interesting exercise."

"So you set the whole thing up. What would have happened if I had just left Cat in the building?" he asked, barely managing to keep his voice civil.

"Then she would have died. We set up the experiment in real space and time. It was no illusion."

"Then are you not guilty of the same disregard for

life of which you accuse humanity as a whole?"

"Silence, do not presume to judge *us.* You are the ones on trial here." A lightning flash sparked from the being's fingertips and he reeled back, clutching his arm, and clenching his teeth against the waves of agonizing white-hot pain

\*\*\*\*

Cat's heart lurched in sympathy as Kerry almost stumbled against her. She reached out her hand to steady him. Pain shot through her whole body, so she nearly lost her balance and fell. She recovered herself, trembling uncontrollably. She glanced again at Kerry. He made no sound but his face was deathly white. She winced. If she'd felt a reflection of his pain, merely through touching him, what must it have been like for him to be on the receiving end of the direct force?

"We have looked into your minds and memories of your past. Despite mankind's inherent selfishness and lack of regard for the sanctity of every life, it appears that, on rare occasions, humans are capable of self-sacrifice and compassion toward each other."

The woman—if such she was—raised her hand once more.

The walls of the room shimmered, seeming to dissolve before the strange, unreal light gave way to darkness.

After a few seconds, the light returned, a pale golden sunlight. Dark pink wisps of cloud drifted across a silver-hued early morning sky. A green, rolling meadow in an alien landscape formed a backdrop for two opposing factions. An unnaturally tall, cloaked albino, stood a little apart from the armed group behind him. Several figures stood facing him, including Kerry and the blond man who now stood, in the flesh, on her right. She glanced across at him. By his bearing, and from her memory of holo-clips she'd seen, she deduced he was the *Destiny's* commander, Jon.

She turned her attention back to the scene unfolding before them. A group of blue-skinned people, shackled together, dug up huge swathes of otherwise un-spoilt land. Overseers goaded them with vicious electric whips.

The albino spoke, but Cat could not make out the words. Her attention locked on the image of Kerry. A slightly younger Kerry, who stood next to a beautiful redheaded woman, dressed in green, her hair falling in soft ripples over her shoulders. *That must be Jess.* As she watched, the mutant reached out and grabbed hold of the woman. She struggled, eventually breaking free, as Kerry lunged toward her. A thin stream of what appeared to be laser fire zapped out, and she plunged forward at Kerry's feet. As he held the dying girl in his arms, his face buried in her hair, the scene before them erupted in a blaze of blaster fire transforming a peaceful vista of grassland into a bloody battlefield.

Cat glanced at Kerry—the flesh and blood Kerry who stood beside her—and cringed inwardly at the anguish she saw on his face. She wanted to reach out to touch him, to show him he did not have to bear this pain alone. However, that would not be a wise thing to do. It would probably anger their captors and she would not risk being the cause of him being hurt again by this strange being's unearthly power.

Once more, her eyes met his as the alien woman spoke again.

"It seems your species is a curious mixture of

compassion and violence. For this reason, we took advantage of your arrival on this planet to set up a series of experiments to determine if a random sample of your kind could convince us there was still hope for you." Again the room became dark before dissolving, leaving them suspended in the void.

Deep space. The beautiful, gigantic ship. The *Destiny*. Then, on the surface, her own escape vessel, crashing on the planet. Scenes of the fight between the *Destiny's* crewmembers, and their unknown assailants, flashed before them. Moments later, the scene shifted to her tending to Kerry's wounds, taking him back to her own vessel, and sharing a meal with him.

"In fact, you both passed the test of compassion we set you," the woman went on. "The next test was to see how you would react when forced to work together. You passed that test too, proving individuals of your species are able to put aside your differences and co-operate when there is a common danger."

Again the darkness, which she now recognized as the prelude to what was almost a holographic picture show, except those were her own experiences being projected into thin air. This time images of their fight with the creature from the river flashed past. Then the scene switched to their time in the small town. It showed them talking that night, then holding each other, hidden in the shadows to avoid being seen by the Union officials, and working together to steal the transit vehicle.

"You conjured up the animal that attacked me at the river?" Kerry asked hoarsely.

"No, that is one of the indigenous species of this planet, although it was a useful addition to our experiment. We set the test to see how you would react when pursued by," she waved a hand toward Shalina and Dorian, "these people who are your enemies, and one of whom," she directed her gaze at Cat, "bears a certain relationship to this woman. We were again surprised when you demonstrated that despite being at odds with each other, you could still work together."

She tried to shake off a sudden feeling of dizziness. The alien's piercing stare seemed to bore straight through her, as if probing every nerve in her body. After a brief pause, the entity spoke again.

"It seems we failed to realize what frail creatures you humans are. You have our permission to seat yourselves."

For the first time she became aware of the presence of a padded bench behind her and sank into its softness. How could she be expected to come to terms with the situation, and the knowledge that everything she had believed for so long was a lie? It was hard enough to realize her sister was still alive, after all this time believing her to be dead and swearing vengeance on the man she believed responsible. Harder still to have to accept that the person she once looked up to, respected, and loved, despite only sharing one biological parent, held her in such contempt. Not only that, but Shalina had taken up with the man who betrayed her and her friends. Her presence here made a mockery of everything Cat previously believed, everything that drove her to seek the *Destiny* and destroy the man who stood next to her.

Her logic told her the woman with Dorian could not be Shalina, despite bearing a striking resemblance to her, allowing for the length of time since they last saw each other. Could Shalina really have escaped from the stranglehold of the Grakks? Was the story she'd told them about her so-called "escape" really credible? From everything she'd heard, anyone transported by that fearsome race to the penal planet of Salmar would be enslaved and brainwashed to such a degree there would be nothing left of the original personality. Perhaps she and Dorian were another illusion conjured by these sinister beings, although the *Destiny's* crew seemed real enough.

Perhaps this was an elaborate mass hallucination, one from which she would presently wake and find herself…where? Maybe she hit her head when her escape vehicle crashed, and everything since then was just a dream born out of delirium, and she still lay unconscious in the damaged craft.

Kerry seated himself beside her. Again, they locked glances, his expression, as usual, impassive. No, this was no dream. She could never have dreamed up eyes like his.

The entity turned to Shalina, Dorian, and the small group of Union officers who stood beside them.

"You are also on trial. You have murdered and stolen and represent everything that is corrupt in humanity. The tests you have undertaken here did not result in you ingratiating yourselves into our favour. You took advantage of the situation the other two defendants found themselves in and seized their companions, taking them prisoner."

Cat's attention turned toward the tall, blond haired man, Kerry's friend and commander of the *Destiny,* Jon Quinlan. Kerry had told her Shalina seduced the *Destiny*'s commander in order to further her plans to steal the ship. It must have been just as much of a shock for him to realize she was still alive, as for her and Kerry. Hard to believe the man, who looked so strong, could have been taken in by a beautiful woman, her own sister, no less. She dismissed the thought as fast as it came. Had she not done the very same thing herself? Love was the biggest deceiver of all. How easily she'd allowed herself to be taken in by Dorian. She'd trusted him, believing him to be honest and as committed as herself to destroying a corrupt regime. He'd fooled her into thinking he loved her, and then betrayed her and her friends to their enemies, leaving her to face the consequences. What right had she to judge someone else for being deceived by love?

****

Again the darkness. Again the *Destiny,* magnificent in the dark recesses of deep space. The scene changed to the interior of the ship, on what must be the flight deck. The sophisticated instrumentation panels and comfortable crew stations were breath taking, but Cat could not concentrate on anything but the figure of Kerry, standing with Shalina. Her hair was different, long and flowing, but there was no mistaking her, even though she'd changed significantly from the girl, barely out of childhood, she remembered. It was apparent from their body language she was attempting to seduce Kerry but he made it obvious he would not allow himself to be tempted.

Another shift of the light and Jon appeared. This time Shalina entwined her arms around him as they talked in soft tones. A moment later, the air shimmered and changed to a different scenario. Kerry and Shalina appeared deep in argument, Shalina scowling and waving her hands as if in protest, while Jon looked on in obvious disbelief.

She glanced at Kerry again, and the scene changed once more, with Shalina racing to the launch bay and boarding one of *Destiny's* ferries

"You betrayed your fellow crew members and tried to steal their ship for another race. Greedy and ruthless, you turned against the man who spurned you, without consideration for how you betrayed and deceived the one who loved you. Even now, you are consumed by greed. You would have felt no compunction in killing him, and any others who got in your way, in the same manner you have killed others of your species. Therefore, you will be punished in a manner we deem fitting."

Neither Shalina nor Dorian spoke. Cat looked across to where they stood, sullen and silent. None of this made sense. How could Shalina have survived torture by the Grakks and be standing beside her in the flesh? And what tests were they set by these judgmental beings, who had the ability to take past events from their subconscious and project them to everyone there? As she watched, a silver mist descended around the two, and they disappeared before her eyes.

The woman's voice again rang through the courtroom. "They will, in due course, be punished for their own crimes. They are not worthy to be judged for the crimes of humanity as a whole."

"And we are? So—are we deemed guilty or not guilty?"

Cat turned to look in the direction of the speaker, Jon Quinlan. "Human, you have seen the consequences of our anger before, do not oblige us to teach you the same lesson we gave your friend." There was a slight pause. "We have not yet reached our decision. Before we decide, we have further tests for these two, whom we have chosen to represent your species. If they succeed in convincing us the human race is worth another chance, you may all return safely to your ship." She paused for several moments before adding, "I see you have questions. You may now lay them before us."

"My companions," Kerry said, "why have you brought them down from our ship?"

"It was important for your friends to witness the trial together. We could have projected this place to your starship, but we wanted them to observe our methods first hand, although for the safety of your ship, we have left the other telepath on board. We need you to send this message to the people on your home planet, and the planets they now control: If you persist in spreading across the universe and destroying other planets and their ecology, as well as your own, you will be punished. It is within our power to eradicate Earth, and any of her allies and colonies who display the destructive tendencies of mankind"

"Then do we have a 'Stay of Execution'?" Kerry asked.

"For the present, if that is how you would like to regard it. We have learned much from your responses to our tests, and have grounds to hope humanity will eventually learn from its mistakes. We already know there are planets occupied by human life forms who respect the natural order of the planets they have settled on and made their home. We do not believe that humanity is a lost cause, which is why we are giving you another chance to redeem yourselves as a species."

"And what does that involve exactly?" Jon spoke again, his voice soft, although it held an underlying tone of resentment. Despite their current predicament, he stood straight and calm, as befitted his status as commander. Again, the thought flitted through her mind that it was difficult to believe such an outwardly strong man had allowed himself to be deceived by her own sister.

She brought herself back to the present as the woman spoke again, looking directly at her and Kerry.

"We will return you and the others to the planet you call Robigo, where your vehicle awaits. On that planet, you will prove whether you have learned the meaning of friendship and loyalty. If you pass this next series of tests you will be allowed to go on your way in peace, and we will reconsider the future of your species." There followed a long pause and her voice grew even sterner and colder. "Should you fail the final test, you will all die, and the fate of the human species will be in great jeopardy."

Chapter Fifteen

Cat bit back a response that these beings, who'd set themselves up as judges and jury, were no better than the people they presumed to judge. What gave them the right to condemn or reprieve the human race? Perhaps she and her companions were merely pawns in a game of distraction for a race of so-called "superior" beings? Or was there a more sinister purpose?

It looked like some of those questions were about to be answered. The room around them dissolved, once more, and swirling mist enveloped them. When it lifted, they found themselves back on the now familiar soil of Robigo.

\*\*\*\*

"So what are we supposed to do now?" Berne asked, "What do we do now?"

"We get back to the *Destiny* as quickly as possible," Jon said. He nodded toward Cat, a glint of curiosity in his eyes. "Are you the pilot of the escape-craft whose distress signal we intercepted?"

"Yes, this is Cat...Kincaid," Kerry said inclining his head in her direction. "Her escape craft was damaged in the crash."

Cat nodded a greeting, unable to find words to speak as he introduced the other three crewmembers. She still felt a sense of shock as she tried to process the events of the past hour or so. She looked around. They were now in an area close to where they'd left their crashed stolen vehicle. It stood as if waiting for them, in no worse a condition than when they stole it.

"I don't believe it. That thing was in flames when we crashed," Kerry said, raking his hand through his hair. He stopped, as if remembering something, and inspected his hand closely. "And the skin was burned off my hand when I tried to beat the flames out on the control panel. There's not a mark on it now, and I haven't used the regenerator. It just doesn't make sense."

"Neither does anything that just happened," Jon said, in his slow drawl. "One moment we were taken prisoner by Union officers, the next we were here. If all that was some kind of hypnotic illusion, we could still be experiencing it."

Cat took several deep breaths. She needed to focus. The more she thought about it, the more likely Jon's theory seemed. She sighed. On reflection, however, the feelings Kerry instilled in her were far too real to be the products of delirium.

"It's a miracle either of us escaped the crash without being killed, let alone seriously injured," Kerry went on. "How could Cat and I both have imagined it?"

"I suggest we worry about that later," Jon said. "The important thing now is to get back to our ferry and return to the *Destiny* without any further delay." He consulted a small device on his wrist. "We're only just over twelve klicks away from where we left it."

After a brief consultation with Jon, Kerry programmed the co-ordinates into the hover-car.

"You think it's wise to use this, after all that's happened?" Cat asked, finding her voice at last. "It might be safer to walk, although personally I can't wait to get away from here."

"We do need to check it first"—Kerry glanced across at her—"in case it's been booby trapped. I don't trust anything on this planet anymore." As he spoke, he ran his small hand scanner across the vehicle's hull.

She nodded. "Too true, we don't want a repeat of what happened at that old building."

Jon shot a questioning look at her and then turned his attention to the telepath. "There seems to be no sign of anything suspect. Do you sense anything Regin?"

Regin stood closer to the hover-car and seemed to concentrate intently for a second or two. Then he stepped back, shaking his head. "I can detect nothing untoward or suspicious. It seems safe enough."

"We came across a ruined building some distance from where Kerry said your escape vessel landed and were exploring it when a device went off and buried us in rubble," she explained, in answer to Jon's quizzical expression. "Kerry got out of it, but I was badly injured and buried beneath a pile of rocks and timber. He dragged me out."

Jon nodded, his features betraying nothing. She stopped and pursed her lips in a low whistle. A patch of undergrowth materialized and revealed itself as the chameleopard. Jon put his hand on his blaster and the others also reached for their weapons. "Don't worry," Kerry said, "it's a friend of Cat's. He is harmless."

Jon and the rest of the crew lowered their weapons, although still casting doubtful glances in the animal's direction. "What are you going to do about him?" Jon asked. "He can hardly travel in the hover-car."

"He'll be fine," Cat said. "He can follow. His

species is very swift. He'll have no difficulty keeping up." She made to seat herself in front of the controls but Kerry laid a restraining hand on her arm.

"I'll take her. I know how to handle her now, and you don't."

He had a point, but it would have been interesting to find out how this strange little craft handled for herself. She frowned. "Suit yourself. We really don't have time to argue. We need to get back to your ferry before we have any more nasty surprises."

Kerry took up position in front of the control panel, and she seated herself beside him, while Berne's wife, Zeldra squeezed in on his other side, with Berne, Jon, and Regin in the back. The vehicle was probably designed for four passengers rather than six. The cramped conditions were preferable to walking out in the open, however, and it would afford some sort of protection in the event of them running across hostile forces or any of the Union personnel.

"You know I still have a bad feeling about all this," she said, turning her head toward Kerry. "You remember you said escaping from the town was too easy? Well it was, and so is this. Those people— Therocians or whoever they are—who put us on trial, it seems they're setting us up for another of their 'tests'. Not to mention the fact this vehicle should be a smouldering wreck."

"We need to watch our backs," Jon said. "I'll be happier when we get back to the ferry and are on our way back to the *Destiny*. It would be foolhardy to relax until then."

They were close to the *Destiny's* transit vehicle, and near enough to see the outline of the ship in the distance through the trees, when they heard a distant rumble like thunder. It grew louder by the second, reverberating through the forest. Moments later, a herd of huge, shaggy animals, with long, curved tusks, broke through the trees, bearing down on them.

"Hold tight," Kerry yelled, "I'm going to take her up a far as I can. We may be in for a rough ride."

Cat experienced a moment of panic, instantly replaced by anger. Were they about to endure another of the Therocians' "trials"?

Kerry obviously struggled to try to gain some height. "It's not responding," he ground out. "I can't get above the trees." She could not help but admire his skill as he tried to dodge sideways through the trees to avoid the herd, while ensuring the craft did not get dashed against the thick trunks.

The monstrous herd rumbled toward them, throwing up a cloud of choking dust and sand. One of them saw the vehicle and lunged up to it, with a howl that rent through the air like the call of a banshee. It reared up on its hind legs and caught the side of the craft with one of its massive tusks, tossing it aside like a pile of leaves. In seconds, the herd thundered into the distance, and the hover-car listed at a crazy angle, with Kerry making a desperate attempt to right it. Cat had a momentary sensation of vertigo as the vehicle spun out of control toward the ground. The huge trunk of a tree loomed before them, and once again, she braced herself for impact.

****

Kerry became aware of a stabbing pain in his shoulder and blood dripping down his face. Automatically, he reached for the control to slide back the roofing panel. Nothing happened. He tried again. He sniffed the air. A caustic smell of burning assailed his nostrils, causing him to cough and his eyes to smart. This time the situation was all too real. There would be no mysterious teleportation to safety. They needed to get out—and fast.

He glanced to his left where Cat slumped forward in her seat, her hair matted with blood. She must have been thrown forward by the impact of the crash and hit the control panel in front of her. Because of the angle at which the craft lay, tilted to one side, he could not see the others. He knew he needed to act quickly. He reached for his blaster and aimed it at the roof canopy, succeeding in making a large hole in it. Thankfully the position of the vehicle at least made it easier to avoid most of the pieces of molten flexi-glass as they spattered around him. He wrenched open his safety harness and used the butt of his gun to enlarge the jagged opening enough for him to crawl through and move to the back of the vehicle. To his relief none of the others seemed severely injured, and Zeldra was already trying to scramble through the broken shield. He extended his arm to help haul her through the hole in the canopy. "Are you all right?"

She nodded. "Yes, just minor cuts and scratches. We were lucky." She stopped, as her glance alighted on Cat's motionless form in the front seat.

"If that is what you call 'lucky'," he growled. "Help me get Cat out. The car could blow any moment."

Between them, they managed to lever Cat out of the vehicle and lay her on the ground. Berne and Regin, who were also now free of the wreckage, hurried over to where Zeldra ministered to the unconscious woman.

"How bad is she?" Kerry asked, his concern for Cat overriding everything else.

"She's stable for now. I've used the bio-regenerator to repair some of the damage, but her breathing's weak and she's lost a lot of blood. We need to get her to safety as soon as possible."

"Like now," Kerry muttered. He lifted the unconscious woman in his arms, ignoring the stabbing pain in his arm and shoulder. They broke across the clearing at the edge of the trees and reached the ferry moments before a massive explosion rent the air and the ground shook beneath them. Kerry rolled over hoping to break the impact of their fall for Cat. Jon reached the ferry first. Kerry laid a restraining hand on his arm before he could initiate the entry sequence via his communicator.

"Not yet," he warned. "The hover-car may not have been booby trapped, but if the Union came across it, the ferry could be. We need to check." He cradled Cat's inert body in his arms. Apart from the pallor of her skin, blood trickled down her face, and she remained unconscious. Fear squeezed his heart in its icy grip. *Not again. Please, not again.*

There was no time to indulge in self-recrimination or guilt. The sooner they were able to enter the craft the sooner they could get to the *Destiny* and give Cat the care she needed. He laid her on the ground and Berne came to his side

"It's all right Kerry, it's all right. We'll take care of her."

Zeldra also knelt beside Cat. He knew she would be in safe hands; they were both skilled medics. It did not make leaving her side any easier but he could do nothing more to help. He joined Jon and Regin. "Do you sense anything Regin?"

"There is something," the telepath said. "Something not natural or consistent with the composition of the craft." He reached down beneath a tailfin. "Here, I think there's a device of some sort here."

Kerry knelt on the hard earth and examined the area carefully. "Yes, a fairly unsophisticated contraption. It's set on a long countdown—but any attempt to access the entry port and it would go up immediately, taking us with it."

"Nice," Jon stated. "Can you deactivate it?"

"Well if I can't, we are in trouble." He lay flat and inspected the device. It should not be too difficult to disable. It would help if his head would stop throbbing though. He'd almost forgotten his own injuries in his anxiety about Cat. After an agonizing few minutes, he finally managed to work out the sequence. He carried out a deft manoeuvre with the small tool from the kit he always carried and breathed a soft sigh of relief as the countdown abruptly ceased.

"That was a close call," he said. "Five seconds more and we would have been history." While Jon instigated the entry sequence Kerry went back to where Cat lay, attended by the two medics.

"Will she be all right?"

"We've done all we can for her, for the moment," Berne said. "She needs to make up blood, and the best place for her is *Destiny*'s sickbay."

"Fine, then let's go," Kerry said. "She sustained horrific injuries when the building collapsed around us, and lost a lot of blood then. Her body must already be weakened."

"She's seems strong," Zeldra said, "and she appears to be a fighter. She's taken a bad blow to the head and is concussed, but the bio regenerator has healed most of her injuries." She touched his arm reassuringly. "Don't worry. We'll do everything we can to get her to pull through."

He nodded, not trusting himself to speak. He took Cat in his arms, and once on board and clear of the airlock, laid her on one of the bunks in the small aft section

"Zeldra will take care of her now," Berne told him, after checking her vital signs and covering her with a thermal blanket. "Let me take a look at you. You're bleeding. You've a very nasty gash on your back and shoulder, and on your head and face. Very nasty."

Despite his protests, Kerry found himself obliged to sit still while Berne ministered to his injuries. His head throbbed where he'd cut it but the shoulder caused him the most pain. The same shoulder he'd hurt when attacked by the animal at the river the day Cat saved him from the creature. He tried not to flinch when Berne ripped his tunic away from his shoulder and applied the bio regenerator.

His mind drifted off and a vision swam before his eyes and refused to be banished back to his subconscious. Jess, who'd saved his life at the cost of her own. This could not be happening again. He could not deny the reality of what he told Cat. Despite the fact he did not believe in superstitions, misfortune seemed to befall any woman who came close to him, and she was obviously no exception.

He sighed inwardly. Perhaps one day he would be free of the pain…the guilt. He'd lost every woman who, like Jess, meant anything to him, including the mother he never knew, or anyone who had more than a passing connection to him. He even drove away Laitha, the brilliant little ecologist and biologist he'd hardly even noticed all the time they worked together on board the *Destiny*.

The youngest member of the crew, Laitha had tried to comfort him after Jess's death. Eventually he made it clear to her he did not intend to ever get close to another woman again. Sometime later, a small ship intercepted the *Destiny*—a ship carrying a woman, the image of Jess, who later confessed to be a shape shifter masquerading as his dead love. The incident had opened up the old wounds, and Laitha announced her decision to obtain passage on a ship for Earth. As soon as they passed close enough to one of the Earth colonies, she left the ship. No one suggested his coolness toward her directly related to her departure. They did not need to. The look in her eyes when she bade her final farewells made her feelings abundantly clear. She might not have been someone he felt very close to, but he had liked and respected her and she was one more woman who had suffered because of him.

When Berne finished his treatment of the wound, Kerry shook himself out of his mood of melancholy and sat beside Jon at the controls. The three hours it took them to reach the *Destiny* seemed like an eternity.

"*Metisa*, this is ferry Zero Three. Open the primary airlock." After a few moments, the female voice of the *Destiny*'s main computer responded with the required, "Affirmative."

Once the ferry was on board, they waited for the pressure to equalize and the inner door to open. As soon as they were able to leave the transit craft and step out to the main flight deck, Kerry took Cat into the turbo lift and carried her to the sickbay where Zeldra and Berne took over.

"You've done all you can, Kerry," Zeldra said, her voice reassuring. "You just have to leave the rest to us. We'll do our best for her, I promise. Until we make a proper examination we can't be sure, of course, but it's likely her body's just taking its time to recover. I believe she'll regain consciousness once her body's completed the healing process initiated by the bio-regenerator."

Kerry had to be content with that. Passing his hand across his eyes and shrugging off the fatigue that all at once threatened to overwhelm him, he made his way to the flight deck. He checked the control panels and computer settings, and ran several system tests and diagnostics.

"Everything seems to be in order," he said at length. "I can see no visible signs of tampering and the instrumentation does not register any either." He turned to the telepaths. "There is something that does not add up though. Delian, Regin, and Zeldra were still on board the *Destiny* when Jon and Berne made planet-fall. How did you get down there without taking one of the other ferries?"

"That's something we'd like to know ourselves," Regin said without expression. He looked at his brother. "Delian and I both felt it at the same time—a sense of great power. The next moment we lost contact with each other, and I found myself down on the planet with

Jon and Berne. A most disconcerting experience, one for which I have no answer. I did not use psychic teleportation, and even if I had, it wouldn't account for the transportation of Zeldra as well."

"Well, it obviously wasn't an illusion, like the 'visions' we saw in their so called 'courtroom'," Jon said. "I would like to know what sort of beings they are, and exactly what their intentions are." He paused. "I almost get the sense they're playing cat and mouse with us. I have a strange feeling they haven't finished with us yet. I wonder what else they have in store." He turned to the others. "Is everyone all right? I think Cat took the worst of the injuries. The vehicle turned over on the side where she was sitting, but how is everyone else?"

"Nothing the bio regenerators couldn't fix," Zeldra said. "Kerry, you need to get some rest."

"I will, as soon as I have set the *Destiny's* course. The sooner we get away from this sector of space the better." He seated himself at the ship's main control panel and turned his attention to the screens. "It must have been quite a shock to see Shalina again," he said, quietly enough for only Jon to hear.

"I thought at first it was part of the illusion. I guess I'm glad to know she's still alive, although it's something of a miracle she escaped from the Grakks…" He hesitated. "I can't help how I felt about her, even though she betrayed me—us—and the ship. She seems even harder now and more ruthless. I think seeing her again has finally laid the ghost to rest." He sighed deeply. "Although I suppose I'll always wonder what we might have had, if she hadn't given into her greed, and lust for power."

Kerry gave a brief nod of understanding. They both had old crosses to bear.

He prepared to input instructions into the main navigation computer. "Are we returning to the same trajectory we were on when Cat's escape vessel sent out its distress signal?"

"I can't think of any reason to change it," Jon said, looking thoughtful. "The sooner we get away from here, the better."

"Except that all at once nothing, including the nuclear core, works." Kerry stepped back from the main control panel in frustration. "The communications systems are dead, as well as the navigation computer and the manual override systems. It would appear we are unable to go anywhere."

Chapter Sixteen

"That's impossible," Jon said, his face impassive. Only his eyes conveyed his concern. "The system is infallible—you know how many fail-safes are in place."

"Nevertheless, the only things working at the moment are the life support systems."

"Well that's *something* to be thankful for. Any idea what's causing the problem?"

"There is no fault with the ship itself. We would know if there were malfunctions in any of the systems." Kerry shook his head and sighed in exasperation. "I suspect it has something to do with the aliens who held us on trial down there. It seems you were right and they have not yet finished with us." He set his lips in an attitude of defiance. "This does not make sense. It will take me a while, but I *will* get to the bottom of it."

"Kerry, you need to get some rest. We all do," Zeldra said, her tone unusually sharp. As the ship's joint medical officers, no one, not even Jon, disobeyed either her or Berne if they issued such an order.

"Zeldra's right," Jon said. "You say you've established it's not a fault of the ship and is something beyond our control. If the ship or her crew aren't in any immediate danger, I suggest we all have something to eat and then get a couple of hours' sleep. Is *Metisa* still functioning?"

"With limited capabilities," Kerry replied. "It is not

available for the normal interactive commands, but the emergency alert system still seems to be functioning and in control of life support."

"Good, then unless there's some emergency we'll meet back here in five hours to see if the situation's changed."

"What about Cat?"

"Don't worry about her," Zeldra assured him. "She's received a transfusion and is stable. The systems were all working at full capacity when we tended to her. She regained consciousness and is now sleeping normally. Rest is the best thing for her. As long as the emergency alert is still operating, *Metisa* will inform us if there's any change. I'll pop in myself from time to time to make sure." She gave him a "don't-argue-with-me" look. "Now go, get some rest."

With some reluctance, Kerry left the flight deck and passing on a meal, went straight to his cabin. He lay down on his bunk. Thanks to Berne, the wound on his head had almost healed, and the one in his shoulder no longer gave him pain. He tried to doze, but despite his exhaustion, sleep would not come to him.

His mind teemed with questions. Who were these alien beings who presumed to judge the humans of Earth? Did the Union have any connection with them? Was Jon really handling seeing Shalina again, or did he just refuse to allow his personal feelings to surface, even in front of him? He counted Jon as one of the few people he could call his friend. They were usually completely open and honest with each other and he could normally tell if the commander was trying to hide his feelings. This time though, Jon was keeping his feelings close to his heart, and he was too weary to try to read them.

His main concern, however, was Cat. A few days earlier, he would have killed her with as little remorse as she would have him. What changed? Would she survive after all she'd been through? She was strong, and Berne swore she would be all right. He had never known the bio regenerator not to work on even the most badly injured personnel. She had lost a great deal of blood but she'd been given a transfusion. She should recover. Why should it matter so much to him? Despite Shalina and Krell's hostile confrontation, why should he believe her assurances about being a double agent who wanted to bring down the Union? She could still be working for the Union while Shalina carried on her own personal vendetta away from the auspices of the main Union hierarchy. If he were honest with himself, he could not deny that, deep down, he wanted her to be telling the truth, and for them to be on the same side.

Finally, he gave up trying to find answers and made his way to the sickbay. He touched a panel on the wall and the area became illuminated with a soft, blue light. As Zeldra said, Cat slept, her face peaceful with a faint flush of pink in her cheeks. Zeldra had sponged the blood away from her hair that now lay spread out over the pillow. He'd only seen her with her hair loose a couple of times. He could not resist reaching out and running his fingers through the soft strands, and pushing it gently away from her eyes. He laid his hand on her brow. Her skin felt warm, but not hot, and her breathing was steady. He studied the data on the life-support panel. It appeared she slept normally, her life functions stable. Satisfied, he left the sickbay, to go back to his own cabin. When he reached it and once more lay down on the bunk, he realized how tired he actually was. He closed his eyes—and finally fell asleep.

\*\*\*\*

When he woke, he found he'd slept longer than he intended. He went back to the sickbay. He might as well check on Cat on the way back to the flight deck. He commanded the computer to increase the light by a few degrees, and as the objects in the room became clearer, he rubbed his hand through his hair in surprise. The bed Cat had occupied earlier was empty.

He looked around the sickbay, deserted save for himself. He called her name softly with no response. "*Metisa*, where is Cat Kincaid?" He had no sooner asked the question than he remembered the system now operated with only limited computer functionality. He studied the control panel, made a few adjustments, and then repeated the question. With a soft hum, the feminine voice of the computer sounded through his personal transceiver. "*The woman to whom you refer is at present on Robigo.*"

"What? How did she get there?" Kerry rushed back to the deserted flight deck. He checked the instrument panels. They appeared to function normally once more. That explained how Cat left, anyway. Once the systems returned to normal, she must have taken a ferry back down to the surface. If this was the case, at least she must have made a full recovery.

He spoke into his communicator, "Cat, where are you? Respond please."

When he received no answer, he tried again with the same result. He remembered seeing her communicator on her wrist in the sickbay. Had she taken it off? Either she'd lost the instrument, or something prevented her answering. In view of her lack of response, it seemed likely she was in trouble. Damn the woman. If she was foolhardy enough to go back to the surface alone, he should just let her take her chances.

"*Metisa*, which of the ferries did Cat take?" He hoped she had the sense not to take the same one they used on their return to the *Destiny*. It needed time to recharge its fuel cells. Cat was an experienced pilot. She would surely think of that. He just needed confirmation that she was not drifting somewhere in space with no power source. "*Metisa*, which ferry is missing?" he repeated, when the computer failed to reply.

"*No ferries are missing. All are secured in the launch area.*"

The reply indicated an impossibility. She would still be on the ship if that were the case. She could not reach the surface without taking a ferry, yet neither the sensors nor the computers registered one of the transit crafts leaving. A quick scan of the ferry launch bay revealed all transit and escape vehicles docked and secure, as *Metisa* indicated.

"If that is true," he said, "how did she get down?"

"*There is no data available to answer your question.*"

"That is not possible. She must be somewhere on this ship—unless, unknown to us, she has a teleporter," he added, his tone ironic. The only people he knew of who could teleport naturally were the telepaths of Earth Colony Niflheim, and this ability was limited to only certain individuals. For two centuries man tried to find

177

a way to teleport safely. Experiments were disastrous. Small reptiles and rodents sent via various teleportation systems ended up horribly mangled and deformed. Even inanimate objects did not successfully retain their original molecular structure. The experiments ceased in the late twenty-second century, and he was certain he would have heard if anyone had actually been successful. There must be some other explanation. Unless...

A sneaking explanation crept into his mind. It seemed likely the Therocians were manipulating events again. He scanned the massed banks of controls and ran his fingers swiftly over the instrument panels. Everything now appeared to be working as normal.

"Confirm the time and method of Cat Kincaid's departure," he commanded.

*"Zero three fifty-five and ten seconds,"* the computer intoned. *"There is no data on her method of departure."*

He checked the on-board chronometer. Less than three quarters of an hour ago. Damn, how could he have slept? He should have stayed with her in the sickbay.

*"Metisa*, is there any possible way anyone could have boarded the *Destiny* and kidnapped her?"

*"Negative. Any attempt at unauthorized boarding of the Destiny would have triggered the alarm system as soon as they entered the airlock—"*

"Yes, I am fully aware of that," he said, making no attempt to hide his impatience. "I need to ascertain if there is any chance the detection and alarm systems might have malfunctioned?"

*"Negative. All failsafes are in place. Security—"*

"Thank you," he interrupted. "Please project the

record of the area of the sickbay where Cat Kincaid was, three minutes before her departure from the ship."

A holographic projection of the sickbay appeared in the empty area of the flight deck. He watched as Cat lay sleeping, saw the slight movement of her chest as she breathed. Then the image shimmered and faded. He zapped a control impatiently. The hologram vacillated and then returned to full intensity. The bed was empty.

Three times he re-ran the recording, zooming in as close as he could when the image wavered, but it was impossible to ascertain what happened when Cat disappeared.

"*Metisa,* please project Cat Kincaid's present co-ordinates."

After a moment, the details flashed up and he swiftly transferred them to his communicator. There was only one course of action. He would have to go down there after her.

****

"Jon?" Kerry spoke urgently into the ship's communicator. He waited the few seconds it took Jon to reply.

"What's up—is something wrong? The alert hasn't gone off—is there a problem with the ship?"

"No," Kerry said, "not the ship. Cat is missing."

"Missing—you mean she's not in the sickbay anymore?"

"She is no longer on board. There is no sign of her and she has not taken a ferry, but somehow she has left the ship."

"But that's impossible. Hold on. I'll be there now."

In less than two minutes, Jon stood on the flight deck and together he and Kerry went over the data and

179

the hologram of Cat in the sickbay and, a few minutes later, the empty bed. Jon shook his head and exchanged a look with him over the unexplained loss of transmission between the time of Cat's first appearance in the projection, and the moment when she disappeared.

"*Metisa* confirms she is on the surface."

"Without a ferry? Who is this woman, Kerry, where is she from—could she belong to an advanced race who have teleportation facilities?"

"I wondered that myself," he said, "but it is highly unlikely. She says she is Terran and I have no reason not to believe her—especially since at one time she claims to have worked for the Union on Earth."

Jon did not attempt to hide his look of surprise. "The Union?"

"I said she *used* to work for them. Apparently, she defected and joined an underground movement to try to overthrow the present regime.

Jon seemed to consider this information for a moment. "Go on."

"Dorian Krell and Cat were lovers, he betrayed her to the Union."

"And you want to go down and find her?"

"What choice is there? I can't leave her there, I owe her that much."

Jon regarded him with a combination of concern and disbelief. "You really do care about her don't you—what happened down there Kerry?"

"I don't want to go into it just now, but I do not believe Cat is any threat to us or the ship. She is not like—"

"Like Shalina?"

He remained silent for a moment. At length, he shook his head. "No, she is not. Shalina was hungry for the wealth she thought the Grakks would give her for this ship. At the time, Cat considered what she did when she worked for the Union to be her duty." He paused again. "She could be in real danger. Unless she really does have psychokinetic abilities, the only way she could have got down there is if the Therocians teleported her in the same way they apparently teleported Regin and Zeldra."

"I have to admit it seems the only logical explanation."

"They were able to take memories of the past from our minds, and project them to each of us, and they said themselves they transported you and the others to the surface. They seem to have powers vastly outside our comprehension. "

"And you intend to go down alone?"

"If there is any chance Cat is in danger, I'll not leave her there defenceless."

Jon rubbed his jaw for a moment before nodding. "You're right. It would be wrong to leave anyone alone down there, but I'm coming with you."

"No, this is my problem, I will deal with it."

"That's crazy and you know it. You won't have a chance against the Union, let alone the Therocians, by yourself."

"I have no intention of hanging around long enough for a confrontation. Once I locate Cat, we will head straight back in the ferry."

"The Therocians may not allow you to. As commander of the ship, I refuse to allow you to go down there alone."

For a moment, his words hung in the air in an uneasy silence. It was rare for Jon to pull rank and even rarer for Kerry to go against him. He had no wish to strain their friendship but he would not desert Cat now. "You can't stop me. Cat is my problem. We have no idea what happened to her or what might lie ahead. I'll not ask you to risk your life for someone who isn't even a member of the crew—"

"Well," Jon said, giving him a knowing look. "She obviously means something to you, and that makes her our problem."

He looked at the commander, and hesitated a moment, before replying, "I did not say she meant anything to me, but she saved my life when she could have left me to bleed to death."

"Have it your way," Jon said with the slightest hint of disbelief in his voice. "While we're arguing we're wasting time. I'm going to wake Berne and Delian. The four of us will go down to Robigo and Zeldra, and Regin can remain here. I won't leave the ship unmanned."

"Provided the Therocians see fit to allow it. If they brought members of the crew down before, they can do it again."

"It's a risk we're just going to have to take," Jon said. "If the Therocians want to bring the crew down they will, whether we're here or not. I'm as keen as you are to find out exactly what's going on down there, and if you're determined to go back, I won't risk you going alone."

Chapter Seventeen

Dawn painted the sky with fingers of pink and gold, illuminating the mist below in ethereal, incandescent pastel shades. They landed the ferry several kilometres from where they had previously made landfall and stepped out, looking around with some caution. Kerry swept his tri-dee viewer over the area, peering through the drifts of low cloud.

The landscape looked different. They put down the transit vehicle at the precise co-ordinates the computer registered as Cat's location, several klicks from where they boarded the ferry after the hover-car disaster. It might be an optical illusion, caused by the distorting rays of the early morning sun, the mist, and the effect of the fading light of the moons visible at this point. Whatever the cause, the area appeared more densely wooded and the hills in the distance looked somehow unfamiliar, as if changed subtly during their absence.

"I've no idea what game these people are playing," Jon said, "but they seem to be able to distort landscapes as well as teleport people through the ether. I'm sure there's no need to tell everyone to be very cautious and keep your weapons handy at all times. Kerry, can you try contacting Cat again?"

"Cat," Kerry spoke urgently into his communicator. "Cat can you hear me? We're on the surface again. Where are you? Are you in trouble?"

No reply. He tried again. "Cat, if you can hear me, respond please."

"It's no use," he said in exasperation. "I encountered the same problem trying to contact the *Destiny* when we had that first skirmish with the Union. It was several days before we were in contact again. I put it down to solar flares, but I am beginning to suspect the Therocians blocked our signals." He took a small instrument from his pack and studied its readings. "The only trace of any life force seems to be in that direction, north east. Come on. I am getting a little tired of standing around doing nothing."

"I wish I knew exactly what the Therocians' plan," Jon said. "I don't like the idea of being a pawn in some cosmic game of chess."

"Pawns or laboratory animals," Kerry muttered. "I begin to wonder what is fact and what is illusion."

An unnatural, warm wind blew across the red expanse of the plain, dispersing the mist and bringing with it a combination of unfamiliar scents and the smell of rain. The sun rose in the sky, and the moons lost their pale luminescence and soon faded from sight altogether.

Then the varied bird life broke the silence, with the equivalent of a Terran dawn chorus, and various roars and rumbles sounded in the distance.

The landscape sloped gradually upwards. He had almost forgotten the gravity here was slightly greater than that of Earth. He'd grown used to it during his previous stay on the planet but now it seemed to wear him down, dragging at his feet. The air heated quickly as the sun rose higher and soon grew heavy and humid with the hot, swirling wind. They walked for almost an hour. The terrain became more and more difficult with small pebbles and rocks strewn over the land as if a giant hand had thrown them at random. They should have reached the area where the Union set up their camp by now.

"Perhaps we should have brought the overlander," Jon said, "But if those co-ordinates are correct we should have found her by now."

They reached a tall, imposing cliff riddled with fissures and caves that forced them to turn west in order to follow its lines.

All at once, an ear-splitting roar rent the air followed by the crash of something tearing through the undergrowth.

As one, they stopped and raised their weapons, pressing against the cliff face prepared for whatever might be about to attack.

"Be careful. There are many dangers on this planet, and most of the animal life appears to be aggressive," Kerry hissed. As the sound drew closer his finger closed on the trigger button, and he held his breath.

"Doesn't sound loud enough to be a herd," Jon said softly. Before anyone could reply a monstrous form, green and gray like the forest from which it emerged, stopped, shrank to the size of a large dog, and gradually took on a form Kerry recognized.

"Shifter," he called as the animal approached. "It's all right, you can lower your weapons, it's Cat's pet wolf."

The creature obviously remembered him. It came to him and sniffed at his hand, looking at the others, its large, golden eyes wide with curious uncertainty.

"I wonder if it knows where Cat is," he said, "if

she's in trouble she may have sent him to find us."

"Except how would she know we were here and not still on the *Destiny*?" Jon asked.

"I have no idea, but I have the feeling we are being observed. This could be another 'test'."

The animal paused a moment, sniffed the air, and then took off at a tangent to the west.

Jon glanced after it, and turned to Kerry. "Do you recognize this area at all?"

"No, the whole landscape has changed since we left it. There are no landmarks any more, nothing to indicate where anything is—including the Union."

"Talking of the Union, I'm surprised we've heard nothing of them. They must outnumber us and their instrumentation would surely have registered our ferry making planetfall. I would've expected to have seen something of them by now."

"They may now be on another part of the planet—I wonder what happened to Shalina and her sidekick though." Kerry stared into the distance. "I suggest we see where Shifter leads us. With luck, he might take us to Cat."

They pressed on across the boulder-strewn landscape. The land became marshy, and several species of amphibious creatures hopped or slithered into the increasingly numerous pools of water, while colourful insects buzzed across the surface. They took care to keep to the firmest ground. Although their high boots kept out the water, he warned them there could be quicksand or any other manner of perils awaiting them if they lost concentration or became careless.

Eventually they left the swampland behind them. The sun rose high in the sky and the air became even more hot and sultry.

"I wonder how much further we have to go," Berne said, mopping his brow. "How much *further?*"

"We're several kilometres from where we originally landed," Jon said. "Perhaps the animal's leading us on a false trail and he's not tracking Cat after all."

A few more minutes walking found them in a clearing, flanked on one side by a high cliff. A tall female figure emerged from a deep crevice in the rock, striding toward them. The chameleopard went bounding up to her

"Shifter! Shifter, I thought I'd lost you." Cat caressed the animal and rubbed it behind the ears. She looked up as if only then becoming aware of the presence of the others.

"Kerry." They stared at each other, as if not quite believing the evidence of their eyes.

"How did you get down here?" he demanded. "Are you all right?" Cat certainly looked all right. Her skin, flawless and smooth, bore no trace of bruising or anything to suggest the injury she recently suffered to her head and face.

"Yes, I'm fine. I've no idea how I got here. I remember the crash, but after that—" She shook her head as if to clear it. "I seem to have been wandering around in a daze for hours."

He studied her closely. She might give the appearance of being physically unharmed, but her eyes betrayed the trauma she'd recently been through.

"According to the archived data on the *Destiny*, you appear to have been teleported down to the surface, in much the same way Zeldra and Regin were."

"Have you any recollection of what happened?" Jon asked.

Cat shook her head. "No, I only remember the crash. Then I woke up here, alone."

She gave Kerry a direct look. "I tried to contact you on my communicator but couldn't get any answer. Then I realized Shifter was missing and I had no idea where he was."

"I'm afraid we had to leave him when we went back to the *Destiny*," he told her. "To be honest he was the last thing on my mind at the time." He glanced at the animal. "We were not sure how badly injured you were and there was no time to look for him. Your injuries seemed pretty severe. He must have been tracking you—he led us straight to you."

"My injuries, you said? Why, what happened?"

"You don't remember being in the hover-car in the path of a herd of stampeding animals?" Jon asked.

She shook her head. "I vaguely remember us all being in the hover-car when it crashed, but nothing after that."

"The main thing is, we've found you and you're safe. Now let's get back to the ferry," Jon said. He stopped and stared at the animal by her side. "What's the matter with Shifter?" The animal stood still, nose pointed heavenwards, trembling and twitching its tail.

A bluish-green light streaked across the sky on the distant horizon, and then came a vivid flash, followed by a sound like an explosion. A deep roaring noise sounded in the distance, while the land beneath them shook. The wind howled and whipped the loose sandy soil into spirals around their legs. "We need to find shelter," Kerry shouted above the noise of the wind.

They raced back the way they had come, bending against the gale, which all at once raged around them, carrying with it twigs, and small bushes torn up by the roots.

"Take cover in one of these caves," he yelled, "we need to get out of the open—now!"

## Chapter Eighteen

They squeezed into one of the narrow fissures in the cliff face. The force of the wind tore up plants and small trees, and hurled them around outside the entrance as if they were particles of dust, while the atmosphere seemed to glow several times brighter than the planet's sun.

Cat glanced around to make sure Shifter followed them in. She activated the flashlight on her communicator, and gazed around the dark interior of the cave. A large black boulder moved slightly and she sighed with relief. She hated the thought of losing him. For much of her time in space over the last couple of years he'd been her sole companion and she'd formed a deep bond with the animal.

She glanced at Kerry realizing he also watched her. She looked away. They were yet again in a difficult—and probably a dangerous—situation. He'd come back to look for her. The fact lifted her spirits, and caused a myriad of thoughts to chase through her mind. He'd come back for her. Did that mean—no, she gave herself a mental shake. It didn't mean anything, why should it? He'd made it obvious he would never stop loving Jess, would never let his heart be broken or risk losing someone he loved again.

She sighed. Hadn't she made herself a similar promise? When this was all over, they would go their separate ways…except she would have to accept the hospitality of the *Destiny's* crew for the time being of course. She'd lost her ship, and unless she could manage to steal that little beauty belonging to the Union…

The thought began to form in her subconscious mind the first time she saw it. No doubt, Kerry would be glad to help her with that idea. He would probably be more than happy to see the back of her.

They moved deeper inside the cave. It widened out a little and they were able to stand in reasonable comfort.

The wind outside refused to cease its relentless roar, like a ravenous animal. Even inside the cave they could not get away from the sound. "It's a piece of luck we found this cave," Jon said. "I wouldn't have wanted to get caught up in that."

"I wonder how far back these caves go?" Berne said. "They could go on for miles—miles."

"I am not sure I would want to go exploring just at the moment," Kerry said. "In fact I will be very glad to get clear of this planet altogether, as soon as it's safe to go back outside."

Delian walked along the cave floor, feeling along the walls. "I don't think it does go any further back," he said at length. "I can sense nothing on the other side of these walls." He flashed his wrist flare across the surface. "There are no signs of any tunnels branching off."

"I am more concerned about the ferry. With all this sand and debris whipping up the chances of it still being intact…" Kerry's voice trailed off and he turned back toward the entrance.

"All at once it is very quiet. I believe it may have passed."

Jon made for the entrance and peered out. "You're right. It seems calm enough now." He came back into the cave. "It appears to have been a meteor air burst. I think it's safe to go back out again. The sooner we get back to the ferry, the better." His face looked grim in the steady light of the flares. "If there's anything left of it."

They followed him to the entrance of the cave and stepped outside cautiously. As far as they could see, the remains of small trees plucked up by the roots, and together with boulders and other debris, lay strewn across the landscape. Jon whistled softly.

"That didn't do the ferry any good. Come on, let's see if there's anything left to salvage. I wonder what range the storm covered."

They walked back the way they had come. The poor visibility in the hot, dust-filled air made it even more difficult to recognize any of the terrain. So much of it had changed. Trees, shrubs, even boulders, lay where they were torn up and thrown down again, as if by some huge leviathan.

As they approached the area where they'd left the ferry, they stopped and gazed in shock. The wreckage of the vehicle lay in a heap of twisted, broken metal, with torn off sections scattered all around. They stared at the devastation for a long moment, without speaking.

Jon shook his head in despair. "Somehow we have to find some way of getting off this planet." He turned to her. "How badly is your vehicle damaged Cat? Supposing it survived, is there any likelihood it could be repaired sufficiently to get us back to the *Destiny*?"

She pursed her lips. "I'm sorry, The Union placed a cordon around it, and even if we could break through, the damage it sustained was pretty extensive. I was lucky not to be injured myself when we crashed. It's adequate for shelter, but it won't fly again."

Jon looked at Kerry. "You're the genius when it comes to space vehicles, is there any chance you could make the necessary repairs?"

"Even if it is still in one piece, Cat said her solar chargers were completely destroyed," Kerry stated, his expression impassive. "I would need replacements, and barring a miracle, it seems unlikely we will find any here."

All at once, the air shimmered and shifted as if viewed through a prism, and walls formed around them. Once more, she and the *Destiny*'s crew found themselves back in the courtroom-like environment and in the presence of the mysterious beings from the previous day.

She bit her lip to stifle the caustic exclamation she wanted to make. *Not again.* Why couldn't these aliens just leave them alone?

"So, humans, you still live, and appear to have some concern for each other. That is refreshing." The tallest woman spoke, but her voice seemed to combine with the voices of the ones on each side of her.

"What more do you want with us?" Jon sounded weary as he answered her. Cat glanced at him and noticed a look of frustration now replaced his usual even-tempered expression. Being the one who usually gave the orders, he did not seem too keen on having to answer to someone else. Especially to someone who appeared to be sitting in judgment on the whole human race.

"Silence. You have been told before. We ask the questions—or do you need another demonstration of our power?"

"It's obvious you are trying to keep trespassers from this planet," Jon went on, seemingly undeterred. "We are not prepared to be pieces in some obscure interstellar game. What are you so afraid of?"

"You presume too much. How many times do you need to be told—we ask the questions? And be assured, we 'fear' nothing. However, perhaps you have earned the right to at least a partial explanation. We will satisfy your curiosity when we deem the time is right. So far you have performed surprisingly well."

"So you have had your fun," Kerry said, his voice chilly. "And you must realize we pose no threat to you. When are you going to let us go back to our ship?"

"We have not finished with you yet. You have proven you can have compassion when it comes to dealing with your own—but there is the matter of the others."

"The others? You mean the officers of the regime they call the 'Union?' They have nothing to do with us. In fact," Kerry said, "they tried very hard to kill us."

"You think we were not aware of that?" she asked. "The petty fights and squabbles between yourselves are further proof of the immaturity of your species. We need to know there is hope for humankind as a whole, and that at least some of you have the potential to outgrow the greed and bloodlust your kind has exhibited from the beginning of time."

"Obviously, you have the power to overcome anything that gets in your way. Why do we bother you so much? Jon asked.

"You are correct. Our capabilities are vast—beyond your comprehension. We have developed powers you could not even imagine. Know this planet is not what it seems. It guards the gateway to another dimension that must be protected at all costs. If forced to defend it, we might have to resort to other than peaceful means, which may include the annihilation of your species. Consider your actions well, humans. The future of your species depends on it."

****

The walls of the so-called courtroom melted away, and the next moment they stood on a vast, grassy plain. In the distance, a herd of horse-like animals grazed. Tall purple mountains thrust themselves skywards. Their jagged contours contrasted with the undulating slopes of the foothills on the western side of the plain. Areas of brilliant emerald green lay in dark patches beside a swiftly flowing river, close to where they stood.

Kerry turned to speak to Jon and realized the commander no longer stood beside him, neither did Delian or Berne.

"It appears it is just the two of us again," he murmured. "Our self-appointed 'judge and jury' are apparently determined to see us get killed—or kill each other."

As he spoke, his communicator crackled and the image of Jon hovered above it.

"Kerry—are you both all right? We're back on board the *Destiny*. It looks like you and Cat are required to complete the next test alone."

"Yes, we just reached the same conclusion. It is

fortunate we know you and the others are safe. How long they will allow us to keep in contact is debatable. I'm not sure what is going to happen, but the scenery has changed again."

"Yes, I know."

"You do? How come?"

"There's no logical explanation. The *Destiny*'s main observation panel was dead when we arrived back on the ship, but it's working now. We can see you and Cat and the surrounding area. The airlocks have sealed themselves. There's no way we can get down there at the moment, and as you say, there's no telling how long the communications systems will operate either, in light of our previous experience."

"I wonder why *we* seem to have the honor of playing out this particular performance?" Kerry observed. It felt like he acted a role on a stage, or he and Cat were now living pieces in a particularly sadistic game of chess. "Stay with us as long as you can."

"Be very careful," Jon warned, and Kerry noted the concern in the commander's voice.

He looked across at Cat, standing patiently, but with a fire of determination in her eyes that defied anyone or anything to cross her. Perhaps it was not such a bad thing he and Cat were thrown together, and in spite of their differences, they'd come to know and co-operate with each other. Indeed, he had to admit their relationship now almost bordered on friendship.

He caught his breath. *Friendship*? Hell, who was he trying to fool? She fired his blood and made his body react in a way he found more than disturbing. Notwithstanding his words to her at the river, after that first kiss, what he felt for her went way beyond the purely physical. Despite everything, he was a hair's breadth away from falling in love with her. If he let himself.

The communicator hummed, cutting the transmission to the *Destiny*. In the same instant, Cat reached for her pistol, and he heard her soft gasp. Two figures, weapons drawn, stood a few meters in front of them. Shalina and Dorian Krell.

Krell shouted. "Keep your hand away from your guns. I want the chip. Now."

*Chip? What chip?*

"I don't know what you're talking about," Cat said, her voice calm, but he noticed she stiffened and blanched visibly. He could not be sure if she lied, stalling for time, but she did not falter as Dorian Krell reached out his hand, waving his blaster in a menacing gesture. He could not quite put his finger on it, but something about the whole situation seemed rather surreal.

"You know exactly what I'm talking about. I suggest you give the chip to me now. If you don't hand it over, I'll kill you." In a swift movement, Dorian sprang close and placed the muzzle of the gun under her chin. "I mean it. And then I'll search every inch of your body until I find it."

A wave of cold fury swept over him. He stepped directly in front of Krell, ignoring the blaster waved in his face, his own weapon aimed at Krell's head. "Kill her and you'll have me to contend with."

Krell's glance shifted momentarily from Cat, to the side where Shalina stood, blaster at the ready.

"Touch that trigger and Shalina will shoot you where you stand."

"We seem to be at something of an *impasse* then, because I *will* fire if I have to. This trigger is very sensitive and the reflex action, if you shoot me first, will result in your own demise."

"You're bluffing"

He and Krell pressed the firing mechanisms of their weapons at the same instant. Nothing happened. Krell tried again and threw down the weapon with a coarse obscenity.

"Shalina," he commanded, his features hardening even more, his mouth twisted in an ugly sneer. "Kill him."

Shalina fired her blaster with the same result as the two men. Krell flung Cat toward Shalina and lunged at Kerry. He pressed the trigger of his own weapon again, in the same instant. It came as no surprise when it again failed to fire. The flash of steel glinted in Krell's hand and he swiftly sidestepped. The other man kicked out and knocked him to the ground, pinning him down with one hand around his throat, his other arm raised to strike. He blinked to clear his head, as the blade descended, and then kicked out hard, sending the knife spinning from his opponent's hand. Before Krell could recover, he leapt up and let loose a blow to the head, sending Krell sprawling.

Out of the corner of his eye, he saw Cat in a hand-to-hand battle with Shalina. He did not know what sort of a fighter Shalina would be, without a weapon, but he was sure Cat could handle herself. In the meantime, he had his hands full with Krell, who regained his feet and launched himself at him once more. He ducked and again aimed for the other man's head with the heel of his hand. Blood spurted from his opponent's nose and mouth. Next moment Krell kicked out and almost knocked him down again, with a vicious blow to the thigh. For a moment pain shot through him, but he recovered and landed a blow with his other hand, followed swiftly by two more. Dorian Krell staggered and fell to the ground. He lay motionless and Kerry knelt cautiously, to check him. He appeared to be out cold.

He felt his blaster hum into life and had the sudden conviction the weapon would not let him down this time. However tempting, he would not kill a man as he lay helpless, and it looked like Krell would be out of commission for quite some time. It seemed they had the Therocians to thank for their situation again. He should have foreseen that the mysterious alien race would disable their firearms—although allowing them to keep their weapons in the first place struck him as somewhat paradoxical. Yet another test of their own integrity, no doubt.

He removed Krell's blaster from its holster and tucked it into his own belt, wincing at the pain in his thigh. After checking the man for further weapons, he looked toward the two women.

Both showed no signs of tiring. Cat fought well. He cast a quick, admiring glance her way. She used the methods of unarmed combat, relying on skill and dexterity rather than strength. Shalina was no match for her, despite being as tall and slightly heavier. She aimed a swipe at Cat's head. Cat ducked, and catching hold of her arm with her body slightly twisted, bent her knee, and threw her over her shoulder. The other woman landed heavily on the ground where she remained motionless.

He approached to where Cat bent to retrieve Shalina's weapon. He knelt over the woman on the ground to satisfy himself that she really was unconscious and not faking, then turned back to face Cat. "Are you all right?"

"Yes, I'm fine, although I don't think these two are in such good shape."

She inspected Shalina's handgun then looked up at him a questioning look in her eyes. "Our weapons are primed and working again. You could have killed Dorian."

"I do not kill in cold blood." Kerry said simply. "There is no satisfaction in killing an unconscious man."

"How did you know their weapons had been disabled?"

He smiled that slow, enigmatic smile. "I didn't. But this whole thing smelled of a Therocian set-up. Krell was right. I *was* hoping I could bluff my way out of the situation." He nodded to the prone forms of Shalina, and Krell. "I suggest we leave them here and ask Jon to send another transporter down here to pick us up." He made an adjustment to his blaster and traced a thin line of almost invisible light around the two bodies. "I've set up a temporary force field. It will keep them confined for a while, and give us time to get off this planet. The rest of the Union contingent will, no doubt, find them eventually."

He spoke into his communicator. "Jon are you there? Can you still hear me?"

"Yes, loud and clear. Quite an interesting fight you had down there. We saw it all. I would be interested in knowing more about the chip they were after, though."

He had not forgotten the chip. He gave Cat a searching look. "Yes, so would I."

"I'll send someone down with a ferry for you, as soon as you give me the co-ordinates—"

Jon's image faded and the communicator spluttered into silence.

A slight sound behind them caused them to turn round simultaneously. Dorian Krell stood, somehow, impossibly, fully armed again, his blaster pointed at Cat's heart. In another instant, he grabbed hold of her, and held her in front of him, with his gun-arm wrapped around her neck.

"Give me the chip, *now*. This time I won't be tricked. And you"—he waved his blaster in Kerry's face—"Throw down your gun, if you want her to live."

Chapter Nineteen

Kerry kept his face impassive. He had no idea what chip Krell referred to, or why it was so important, but he needed to divert Krell's attention away from Cat.

"You are wasting your time with her. She no longer has the chip. I do. I have not had the chance to decode the data on it yet, but it obviously has some value for you, so perhaps we can negotiate?"

"Kerry, don't—" Cat's words were cut short as Krell jerked upward on her throat.

"So *you* have it, do you?" Krell turned to glare at him, still keeping the gun trained on Cat. "I said drop the gun and hand over the chip. You'd better not be bluffing, or she dies."

"Kill her, and I promise you will never see the chip." He laid his blaster on the ground while making a swift calculation of the distance between him and Krell. Could he risk trying to distract him enough to disarm him?

"How do I know you really have it?"

Seeing he had Krell's interest now, he continued stalling wildly, and hoping he would turn his attention from Cat to himself. "I'll show you." He reached toward the left hand pocket of his tunic and looked at Krell for assent. When Krell gave a slight nod, he slowly withdrew a small metal case. As the other man reached out to grab it, he stepped back holding the

202

object high out of his reach. "Before we discuss my terms, and just out of interest, what exactly is on it that is so valuable?"

"You mean you don't know?"

"If I did, I would not be asking."

A smug grin spread across Krell's face. "Didn't you think to ask her? No? Too bad. Now, hand over that chip, or she dies."

"Do you really think this is worth killing for?" Kerry curled his lips in a scornful half smile. "If it means so much to you, go and get it." As he spoke, he threw the small object as hard as he could on to a patch of verdant green, where it settled on the surface.

Krell gave a yell of frustration, and, after a moment's hesitation, flung Cat to the ground, and plunged across the stretch of what looked like luxuriant green vegetation.

"Don't be such a fool. Don't you realize that's quicksand?" Kerry's words were cut off by a piercing yell as Krell lost his balance. Arms flailing, he slowly sank.

Sucked into the ooze, his self-confident expression changed to one of terror. "Help me—get me out of here!"

Kerry lay flat at the edge of the swamp. "I should let you sink," he hissed between clenched teeth, "but I'd much rather kill you in a hand-to-hand fight than see you smothered in quicksand."

The man struggled, sinking even further.

"Don't move. Stay as still as you can. You need to try to lie flat on the surface—" The incessant wind lashed across the surface and whipped his words away.

"Please, help me. You can't let me drown in here."

"You won't drown. You can free yourself if you keep still. Stop panicking. Now…try and lay flat on the surface." He shouted the same instructions he'd given Cat when she found herself trapped in the quicksand, but either Krell could not hear or was incapable of following them, and struggled all the more.

Damn the man, he would have shot both Cat and himself a moment ago. Why should he waste time trying to save him? He looked around for a thick branch he could cut into a plank, but saw only a few shrivelled up shrubs too slender and brittle to support a man's weight. Against his better judgement, he lay flat and reached out his arm, but his six foot two frame fell short of reaching Krell by more than a meter. He glanced to his left as Cat scrambled to her feet

"Cat, lie down and grab my legs."

"What? You want to save him when he would have killed us both without blinking?"

"There is no time to argue about it—just do it."

For a moment, he thought Cat would refuse. She muttered something he did not catch, then her hands grasped his legs, and he stretched out even further across the ooze. Behind Krell, an undulating ripple in the green became more of a wave than a ripple, and Cat gave a low cry of horror.

A wide, flat head broke the surface, with four waving antennae ending in round, bulbous eyes at the end of a long body, as thick as a tree trunk. It looked like a colossal sea slug. When it opened its mouth, it revealed two rows of sharp, jagged teeth. Krell shot a look over his shoulder, and let out a half-strangled yell of terror as he took in the new danger.

Kerry reached for the blaster at his side with his

free hand, and extended the other to the limit, stretching his body across the surface as far as he could. The strain on his muscles became almost unbearable, and he could only hope and trust Cat would not lose her grip on his legs. As he managed to free his blaster from its holster, and let loose a bolt at the monster, Krell made a desperate effort to grab hold of his outstretched hand. The quicksand already reached his shoulders. His terrified struggling to free himself and escape the huge reptile only caused him to sink deeper. Before he could grasp Kerry's hand, the creature struck like a monstrous snake, burying its fangs in his shoulder.

Even as he fired the blaster, trying to avoid Krell, the creature pulled the man under and the quicksand closed over him. Both he and the monster vanished beneath the surface leaving it as smooth and green as if it had never been disturbed.

****

It took all Cat's strength to drag Kerry back but at last he kicked free of the menacing ooze, and they lay together, exhausted on the ground. Kerry reached out for Cat's hand and drew her toward him.

"Thanks. I'm grateful you hung on, rather than letting me get sucked in as well."

"That would've been a bit stupid considering you're my ticket off this wretched planet," she said, trying to keep her tone light, and resisting the temptation to move even closer to him. "Why did you pretend you had the chip though? I'm certain Dorian would've had no qualms about shooting me, but he wasn't interested in you. You could have left me and got away—"

"Yes, I could have, couldn't I? Somehow it did not

seem to be an option, at the time."

Kerry let go of her hand. He rolled over and rose to his feet, blaster at the ready. He scoured the surrounding area. "Forgetting him for the moment—what's happened to your sister?"

"That's strange." She sprang to her feet and looked around, seeing nothing but an expanse of empty grassland. "She was lying over there, unconscious, when Dorian came up behind me and pulled his gun on me."

"Well then, it seems she recovered consciousness and made her escape while I was trying to save your ex-boyfriend."

"I thought she was still out of it—she landed pretty hard," Cat admitted.

"Not to mention the force-field I put around them. It should not have discharged already, I don't like having my enemies hiding out somewhere or possibly lurking in ambush." Kerry put his tri-dee viewer to his eyes and scanned the area. "There is no sign of her. She appears to have vanished into thin air."

"Perhaps the Therocians have her."

"It is possible. They seem to enjoy teleporting people from one place to another. Of course she may just have beaten a hasty retreat when that evil looking worm appeared"

"Worm? You call that a worm?" she shuddered. The thing bore too close a resemblance to a gigantic snake for her liking. She wrinkled her face in a frown as she remembered his earlier action. "Just out of interest, what was it you really threw into the quicksand?"

"Only a micro-case containing a spare communication chip. I always carry a few spares just in case—not that they were of much use when we were unable to communicate with the *Destiny.*" He held her gaze with his own. "I think it is about time you told me exactly what the chip is, and how you come to have it."

She gave him a slight smile before meeting his eyes. "What you told Dorian was half true. I don't actually have the chip anymore."

"What?"

"I knew if he found out about it he'd try to get hold of it. Although, it never occurred to me that Shalina would be involved." She hesitated, and looked away for a moment before continuing, not sure how he would react to the information she was about to impart. "I destroyed it—after I was able to enlist the help of a sympathetic cyber-physician to upload the information to my cerebral cortex. I was determined not to lose the data or let it fall into the wrong hands. My memory now holds all the information that was in the chip."

She watched Kerry's face, trying to read his expression without success

"Go on," he prompted, "what exactly makes it so important, and how did you get hold of it in the first place?"

She might have known he'd want the whole story "After Dorian betrayed us, I helped some of the survivors to get away, as I told you. The leader of the underground movement was an elderly man called Zorick." She paused again. "He was injured in the affray. He didn't make it. Before he died, he gave me the ring he always wore and told me not to let it get into the wrong hands. He'd had the chip embedded in the metal." She met his questioning gaze.

"And what was on the chip? Or is it something you

would prefer not to tell me?"

"I don't see any reason to keep it a secret now—from *you*, anyway." *How ironic was that?* Not long ago, he would have been the last person she'd have revealed this information to. Now she would trust him not only with this secret, but also with her life. "It contains the names of all the senior members of all the groups in our movement, along with locations of the other groups on Earth and other sympathetic planets. Also, the deposit and withdrawal codes for the credits the groups have raised to purchase weapons and services from any organization willing to help us—quite a large sum. One day the resistance groups will be strong enough to be able to band together to overthrow the Union, and they'll need this information. You can see why Shalina and Dorian might have wanted to get hold of the data. The Union would pay a small fortune to obtain it."

"No doubt. I understand why you would destroy the original chip, but why upload it to your own brain and put yourself in danger?" he asked, with his eyes darkening and something she almost felt could be concern in his voice.

"I've asked myself that on more than one occasion. I promised Zorick I would keep the information safe in case it was ever needed. Once I'd ingratiated myself back into the Union's ranks, I took the first opportunity I could to upload the information from the chip. I just wanted to keep my promise to him." She looked away, before continuing, "You're the only person who knows."

"No one will ever hear of it from me, I give you my word. I would like to know how Krell and Shalina came to know about the chip though."

She could not suppress a bitter sigh. "I can only think Dorian would have had no compunction in torturing any of the survivors who were unable to get away—I heard many stories to that effect after I escaped. There were injured and dying all around us when Zorick passed the ring to me. One of them could have seen him and heard what he said. I can't think of any other explanation, but I now know Dorian would stop at nothing to get the information and make a name for himself."

"You seem to be dealing with his demise remarkably well. After all, you and Dorian have a history…"

"After all he's done, after the way he betrayed me and our group, there is no way I could still love a man like that."

"But you *were* in love him."

She hesitated again. "I thought so, at the time. I'm not as forgiving as your friend Jon. I can't forget what Dorian did to me. He hurt me very deeply, and betrayed my trust and my friends. He killed anything I may have felt for him."

****

The fact she trusted him enough to confide her secret to him, a secret that actually made her very vulnerable, must surely mean something. But could he allow himself to believe she would ever trust him completely, or return the feelings he found increasingly difficult to deny? He knew all about trust, or rather the lack of it. It took a long, long time for him to learn to trust women after Shalina's treachery, and the love of a genuine, selfless woman like Jess was the only thing capable of restoring his faith. How could he expect Cat to open her heart and give her trust to any man after all she had been through? He was beginning to realize that beneath the bravado was a far more sensitive, vulnerable woman than the one she tried to project.

"Do you think the crew of the *Destiny* saw what happened?" she asked quietly,

"What—you mean the incident with Shalina? There is only one way to find out. He touched his communicator. "Jon, can you hear me?"

There was no answer. "Obviously the Therocians are back to their old tricks, unless it really is solar flares causing the problem," he said. "I assume the *Destiny's* observation panel would be out of action when all that happened." He ran an impatient hand through his hair. "Until we can get back in touch with the *Destiny,* we can't ask them to launch a ferry to pick us up. In some ways it is a pity the Therocians don't just teleport us back to the *Destiny* like they did the others."

"Careful what you wish for," Cat cautioned. "I don't like these powers of teleportation they have, I prefer mechanical means to get from 'A' to 'B'."

He turned to make a response and drew in his breath.

Cat had vanished.

Chapter Twenty

Kerry passed his hand across his eyes and looked around. Was he the one being delusional now? She could not have just disappeared. "Cat," he called. "Cat, where the hell are you?" Nothing but silence answered him. He appeared to be completely alone.

In desperation, he spoke into the communicator. "Cat—Cat answer me, damn you." Silence. "Jon, Berne, if you hear me, answer. Please—anyone?"

More silence. Something moved against his leg. He drew his blaster and then lowered it again. The shadowy form of Shifter stood at his side.

"I wish you could talk," he murmured. "Perhaps you know what is going on here." He gazed into the distance. "I suppose the Therocians are 'testing' us yet again. There must be a reason why they left me here." The creature inclined its head and Kerry could have almost sworn it understood his words.

He fondled the animal behind its ears. "Well, Shifter, it does not appear I will be transported anywhere anytime soon, and I have no intention of hanging around here waiting for something to happen. Perhaps if I keep walking I will eventually find Cat again." He made a few calculations on his scanner in the hope of picking up Cat's DNA signature, or any indication of intelligent lifeforms. The indications were negative and he shrugged, and followed the chameleopard that loped ahead of him, as if it knew which way to go. Perhaps it could pick up Cat's scent, like a Terran dog and lead him to her, as it did once before.

He tried his communicator again. "Jon, Delian, Regin, can anyone on the *Destiny* hear me?" His only response was complete silence. He considered whether to continue walking or turn back. It seemed obvious the Therocians were planning another test for him. He stopped by a large pinnacle of rock. Before him, a shallow bank of gray shale led down to a small open space below. He looked down at Shifter. The animal faded into the yellowish gray of the earth around them until it became almost invisible. If he looked really hard, he could just about see the contours of its body.

It was a great facility. If he did not know of its presence, he would have assumed he was looking at an empty expanse of land. If only it were possible to devise a gadget to enable a person to blend into the background in this way, similar to a cloaked ferry or transport ship. It was one thing to manipulate the molecular structure of inanimate objects—living creatures were something else entirely.

*What was that?* It sounded like a sharp cry of pain, or perhaps surprise. He whirled around, his hand reaching for his blaster.

He lowered the weapon and swore in frustration. Shalina—a little way in the distance, and she was not alone. She and Cat were once more engaged in a desperate confrontation. Neither woman seemed to see him as they circled each other, ready to make a fatal strike. Cat could handle herself, but how long could this go on? Was she fated to replay this sequence again and again?

Shalina bent to pick up a small rock, aiming it at Cat's head. He raised his blaster again, taking careful aim at the woman. He had to be very careful to avoid hitting Cat. If he aimed for Shalina's leg, the blast would take the limb off, but she would live—long enough to stand trial for her crimes, anyway. He pressed the trigger button. Nothing happened. He tried again with the same result, and put it back in his holster with an oath. Damn these Therocians, what were they playing at now? How could he prevent Cat being killed, or seriously injured, if he did not even have a weapon he could use? As he watched, Shalina's arm stopped in mid-air, and both her movements and Cat's slowed. He had the impression of watching the scene in slow motion. The air shimmered in a way he recognized, and the two figures froze, as if turned to life-sized statues.

He skittered down the bank of shale toward them, then stopped and blinked as several figures formed in the scintillating light. Gradually a single entity materialized fully, although the others remained hazy and indistinct.

"Your weapon is useless," she said, in a voice devoid of expression. "What is it that makes you humans reach for a weapon of destruction in almost any situation of conflict? It seems you have never bothered to master the art of negotiation."

"You possibly have a point, but haven't you finished with us yet?" He tried to keep the note of frustration from his voice. "What is it this time? When are you just going to let us get back to our ship?"

"When we believe you have learnt how to deal with your own violence, and when we feel you and your kind are no longer a threat to the secret we are committed to protect."

Presumably, she meant the planet, Robigo. This chunk of cosmic rock that did not appear to be particularly advanced technologically and offered no mineral resources. Kerry shook his head in exasperation. The whole situation seemed to get crazier with each new development.

"And how do we convince you?" he asked, with a shrug of impatience, "and what have you done with my companions?"

"They are safe—for the moment. We have one final test. One we hope will tell us whether your race has any shreds of humanity left, or whether you are merely creatures so filled with greed and avarice for material things and your own self-preservation that nothing else matters."

That sounded ominous, and what did they mean—his companions were "safe for the moment"?

The air shimmered once more and darkness covered the landscape. "What do you see?"

He gazed at the heavens. Before him glided the starship, so close he could see every detail, every port, every registration mark…even her name. The *Destiny*.

"What do you see?" The entity repeated.

"My starship—our starship, the *Destiny*."

"Tell us about her."

He did not like her tone. "Why do you need to know? Let my companion go and I will give you any information you require."

"Silence—we make the demands. If you wish her and your ship to survive, answer our question."

"She was built in the Terran year 2275," he said,

swallowing his anger. "She was designed by myself and built on the moon. The finest engineers and computer engineers were assigned to her construction, which was financed by Jon Quinlan, her commander."

"And what position do you hold on the crew?"

Hell, this began to sound like an inquisition. He kept his tone as even as he could. "I am second-in-command, although each member of the crew is of equal importance."

"Is that so? But you designed the ship. Without you, she would never have taken form or been the ship she is. No doubt a similar vessel would eventually have been built, but you know any other design would have been inferior to yours."

"I do not dispute the fact."

"Then why is Jon Quinlan the commander and not you?"

Kerry grew impatient. "You took episodes of the past from our minds. If you can see into my past, why can you not extract the information for yourself?"

The figure in the light seemed to grow larger, to pulsate with a glowing red aura. "You will not be told again, we ask the questions. It is for you to give us answers. Now, I repeat. Why does Jon Quinlan command the Starship *Destiny*, and not yourself?"

Kerry forced himself to take a deep breath, feeling his temper rising to the surface. "We agreed from the beginning. Jon financed the whole operation from his considerable personal wealth and with the additional backing of many others from various parts of Earth and the colonized planets."

"And what did they hope to get for their investment?"

"The satisfaction of financing a unique exploratory venture, the promise of a share of any mineral wealth we discovered—which promises we have kept—and for the two medics, the chance to come aboard as crew members."

"And is your relationship with Jon Quinlan purely business?"

Just what were they inferring? "We are friends. Close friends," he said with some heat, "As are all the crew members. Jon and I have known each other for a very long time, since we were young boys, in fact."

"We understand. So you would do anything to prevent harm from coming to him?"

"Of course—or any of the other crew members. What are you getting at? They are all my friends. We look out for each other." He paused. "What have you done with them? If any harm comes to any of them—"

"You wish to see them? They are all on board the *Destiny*. Where else would they be?"

The great ship seemed to glow with a pearly, incandescent light. Then the hull dissolved, the bulkheads became transparent. He stood on the flight deck, although common sense told him that could not be so.

*He was still on Robigo. He could feel the planet's unceasing hot wind on his face.*

His consciousness floated around the familiar equipment and controls. The crew went about their usual routines. He breathed a sigh of relief. At least, if this were a true reflection and not an illusion, they were all safe and unharmed. He glanced at the observation panel. The image it relayed showed a leafy version of this area of Robigo. He and Cat walked together by a sparkling river, Shifter trotting alongside. Occasionally one of the crew would glance at the screen, but the scene was obviously so familiar to them now, they paid it little attention.

"But the image they are getting is false. Why are you showing them images which are merely illusions—and how do I know the images I just saw of the *Destiny's* crew were genuine?"

"Have no fear. The crew of your ship is on board exactly as you saw them. We showed the false image to your companions to avoid making them unduly concerned, and to ensure they do not try to send out a search party for you."

"Why would that bother you? From what we've seen so far, you could easily prevent them launching a ferry."

"Of course, but we have our reasons. Do not question our intentions." The entity waited a while before going on, "Since we have cut off communications between you, they have no choice but to wait until the systems are restored. We have implanted in their minds the fact you are safe and will return when you are ready."

"So what is this all leading to? You said something about another test? How long is this going on? And what have you done with the woman who was with me?"

"Silence. You will not question this tribunal. All will become clear in a moment."

The *Destiny* faded from view. The sky darkened for a moment, and when it lightened again, Cat and Shalina stood still, frozen in time. Only now, he overlooked a deep abyss, and they stood on the very edge on the opposite side. Beneath them, a roiling river of fire blazed in lurid shades of crimson, and white-hot jets of flame flared and licked at the rim. Huge, unearthly creatures with flaming horns, open jaws, and long, snapping fangs, leapt half out of the flames in the blazing depths. Their lashing tails and scales glowed with an unearthly radiance, as if part of the inferno itself. *If Hell really exists, then this must surely be its mouth.*

"You said you would do anything for your friends and to preserve the ship you hold so dear. Now is your chance to prove it."

He did not like the direction this conversation seemed to be taking. His intuition told him whatever they had in store for him would not be good.

"What do you want me to do?"

"It's really very simple."

All at once, he found a small device in his hand, although he had no recollection of how it got there.

"All you have to do is activate the control on the device. The two females will be released from the time lock we have placed around each of them and will fall to their deaths.

"No!" He almost flung the device at the entity before him.

"I won't do it. I will not kill the woman—" He almost said, "...the woman I care for," but stopped himself in time. He did not know if Cat, in her frozen state of immobility, could hear him or not, but if he were ever to confess his growing feelings for her, it would not be like this. Furthermore, he would not show any weakness before the Therocians.

"I will not kill this woman who has saved my life."

"So, you would prefer to sacrifice you friends and your starship. That is easily done. I have only to wave my hand—"

"No!" The anguished cry was wrenched from him. How could he let them destroy the *Destiny*, the culmination of his and Jon's childhood dreams, and with it her entire crew? How could he even contemplate the death of his closest friend, or the rest of the crew, who were also his friends? He could no more allow this cruel entity to kill his companions and destroy his ship than he could blow them up with his own hands. And if he did not prevent their destruction, he would be just as guilty of their murder.

"Then you wish both the women to die?"

He closed his eyes, dark despair filling him with a pain that was almost physical. *Not again. It could not happen again.* Shalina deserved whatever punishment the Therocians meted out to her, but he would not let another woman he cared for lose her life.

"No. No, of course not," he almost spat out.

"Make your decision quickly then. We grow impatient. Will you save the woman, or your ship and the crew it carries? It would seem an easy choice. If you do not make it immediately, they will all die."

The cold, impassive voice held no emotion. He had no doubt she would carry out her threat.

"If your need for blood must be appeased, take me instead. Kill me and let the others go." His voice shook. Never before in his whole life had he begged for anything. Closing his eyes for a moment, for only the second time in his life, he prayed. A prayer that he could somehow save the woman he had grown to love, along with his friends, his fellow shipmates.

His voice to his own ears sounded hoarse with the emotion he did not even try to repress. "Kill me," he repeated, "and let the others live. I beg you, let them live."

"You would give your life in their place?"

He did not hesitate. "Yes, is that not what I just said?"

An unbearable flash, comparable to the most vivid sheet lightning, then a burning shock like a laser bolt hit him with such force he crumpled to his knees. He heard a scream and Shalina fell, as if in slow motion, into the flaming pit below and the jaws of the fiery monsters.

*So he'd sacrificed his life in vain. Had they also destroyed the Destiny and killed Jon and the rest of the crew? And what about Cat?*

Searing pain enveloped him, and as if a severe electrical current seared through his body, he shook uncontrollably and fell backward. For a moment, he imagined he looked into Cat's gray eyes, then the world fell away, and he spun off into space and black nothingness.

Chapter Twenty-One

Cat passed her hand across her eyes in an effort to dispel an overwhelming sense of shock and nausea. Surely, this must be a dream, but it was more vivid than any of her previous nightmares. Sandy soil pressed against her skin. She lay not in a bunk on a starship or escape vehicle, nor even in Kerry's little tent, but on the hard, sandy ground, out in the open—and in broad daylight.

She remembered Kerry standing on a rise opposite her. Below her, a fiery pit, full of indescribable, impossible monsters. Then Kerry bargaining with the Therocians for her life—and the lives of her sister, and the *Destiny's* crew. A tremor went through her body as she recalled, with increasing clarity, the events of the last few minutes. Shalina. Her sister's screams echoed through the confusion in her mind, and she relived the moment Shalina fell into the hideous jaws of the monsters in a flaming pit like the gates of Hell. A groan sprang unbidden to her lips. Shalina did not deserve the horrendous death she'd just witnessed. No one did, and she had been moments away from sharing the same fate.

She stood and tried to cast the thought from her mind as she looked around. She was alone in the desolate landscape. She'd almost hoped the events of the last few minutes were an illusion, that Shalina still lived, and somehow she could get through to her, make her realize… She shook her head, clenching her fists by her side. *Don't be stupid. Shalina would have killed you without a second thought, sisters or not.* Whatever Shalina suffered at the hands of the Grakks had changed her beyond all recognition. The sister she loved as a child bore no relation to the woman who'd threatened her and Kerry so recently. And what had happened to make her lust for power and wealth enough to try to capture a ship like the *Destiny* for an alien race?

Fear gripped her heart, overriding the sense of sorrow and loss, as she realized she stood alone in an area she did not recognize.

There was no sign of Shifter. Had she lost him as well? He usually stayed close to her. And Kerry? Where was *he*? Another strand of memory drifted into her consciousness, like a wisp of smoke from a dying ember. *Kerry*! What had the Therocians done to him?

A sense of dread took hold of her and she shivered in apprehension. Fully alert now, she realized the chasm with the raging furnace no longer existed. The ground where she stood fell as a gradual slope, ending in a narrow fissure, stretching as far as she could see in both directions. She took a cautious step forward and then jumped back in horror. The shallow gorge writhed and squirmed with a mass of snakes, scales glinting in the sunlight. They slithered up the sides, sliding into every crack and crevice in the sandy soil in a way that seemed almost liquid, only to re-emerge nearer the edge where she stood. She bit back a scream, her attention drawn beyond the hideous reptiles to the ground on the opposite side.

Kerry lay there, sprawled on his back, motionless. She could not tell if he still lived or...

No, she would not let herself pursue that line of thought. This man, whom she once swore to kill, had offered up his own life to save his friends—and her. Had he indeed paid the ultimate price? She shook her head in denial.

"No," she said aloud. *No, please, please don't let him be dead. Please, let him live.* She sucked in her breath as she realized how close he lay to the edge. If he was still alive, he had only to move a fraction and he would slip over into the pit of snakes.

She must find a way to get to him. She needed to know if he still lived or...she would not contemplate the alternative. There had been too much death. She'd lost everyone who ever meant anything to her. *Please, not Kerry too.*

She looked around, desperate to find some way across. She squared her shoulders and took a deep breath. She had to go to him. If he was hurt, she might be able to help him. *Please let him still have his bio-regenerator.* Suppose she could do nothing for him? *No, don't think like that.* There was little point in staying here contemplating the worst, when every minute might mean the difference between life and death. She had no choice. She would have to cross the snake-infested pit.

She shuddered again. Snakes! The one thing that would normally have her heading in the opposite direction as fast as she could run. Now her only option was to face the loathsome creatures—or desert the man who'd been willing to sacrifice his life for her and his friends.

She did not even know if the snakes were venomous, but she would not take any chances. Acting on instinct, she stretched her leggings over the tops of her boots, hoping the flexible synthehide would be enough to offer some protection from their fangs. To her relief she still had her emergency pack. At least the Therocians had not deprived her of that. She rummaged around until she found one of her scarfs and tied it around her head and mouth, to protect her face as much as possible. She pulled on her tough working gloves and drew her pistol. She made several adjustments to the weapon and, clenching her teeth, started down the incline, toward the narrow ravine.

She reached the edge and peered down the shallow incline. Her courage almost deserted her and she took several more deep breaths to calm herself.

She fired into the simmering, churning mass. A streak of energy burned a narrow line down the width of the chasm, and the reptiles shrank away. She fired again about half a meter away. Flames leapt and flickered on both sides of the path she'd made. With violent hisses, the snakes recoiled further, and slithered away from the heat. She hoped it would be enough to stop them striking before she could get across. She would have to be swift in order to make it to safety. She trod carefully, with several sidelong glances at the serpents. She dare not run for fear of attracting their attention and causing them to attack. At any moment, she expected to feel one of the reptiles entwine itself around her body or strike, its fangs injecting poison into her flesh. She was almost at the far side when to her horror she realized several snakes had crossed the path she'd laid with her pistol and now writhed around her feet. She felt a thud on her boot, as one of the reptiles struck, followed by another. She glanced down to see one of the vile creatures coiled around her boot.

She lashed out with her foot and kicked it away from her as far as she could. Immediately the others turned to attack it, rolling in a seething, writhing tangle of gleaming reptilian bodies. She approached the rim of the shallow crevice and leapt.

She landed, half crouched but on solid ground, with a low sigh of relief at being free of the snake pit. Kerry still lay motionless. She sprang to his side, and using all her strength put her hands under his arms and pulled him back from the edge. She knelt over him, breathing heavily, then gasped in horror as she spotted another of the snakes. It must have come with her out of the fissure, and now poised, ready to strike at the area of Kerry's arm exposed by his rolled up sleeve.

Without pausing to think, she reached out with her gloved hand and tried to repress the cold fear seeping through her, threatening to freeze her muscles and prevent any movement. Doing her best to hold back her revulsion, she grabbed the snake at the back of the head. Without looking at its wicked, open jaws, and long, curved fangs, she flung it back into the crevasse, and rising, adjusted her weapon again to fire bolt after bolt, until the snake infested fissure flared in a wall of vivid green flame, emitting a pungent smell of burnt flesh.

She holstered her weapon and knelt beside Kerry's motionless form once more. Memories haunted her mind of the first time she'd seen him in person. He'd been unconscious then too. Only on that occasion, she hadn't cared whether he lived or died. Now every cell in her body cried out for him to live. For a moment, she feared she was too late. She pulled the scarf away from her face.

"Kerry come back, don't you dare leave me here alone." Hot tears fell from her eyes unheeded and splashed on his face. She laid her head on his chest. The faint beating of his heart, and the barely discernible rise and fall of his chest, told her he still lived. She took his wrist and felt his pulse, weak, but a pulse, nonetheless.

As she reached into his hip pocket to retrieve his bio-regenerator, he opened his eyes and stared straight into hers.

\*\*\*\*

Kerry passed through the blackness and revolved in a seemingly never-ending vortex of swirling, rainbow colours. Down and down, in a slow-motion descent as if he were being sucked into oblivion. Was this what death felt like? He would have expected nothingness, eternal nothingness. Not this jumble of memories and regret.

Regret, regret for all the things he had not done and wished he had. Things he *had* done, things he wished he had not. Most of all, regret he had no chance to say goodbye to his friends—and to the woman who had come to mean more to him than he could ever have believed possible. The woman who stirred feelings in him he had thought were buried forever in the past.

*"Kerry...Kerry, what have they done to you? Come back. Kerry, don't you dare leave me here alone."*

Her voice echoed as if from a dozen underground tunnels, from so far off he could surely never reach her. How could he hear her voice if he was dead? Had she died too? Were they in some kind of hellish, spiritual other world?

Something warm and wet splashed on his face. *What the ...?*

He tried to open his eyes. The blackness slowly lifted and he found himself looking, as if through a smoky haze, into the eyes that were the object of his last conscious thought before the darkness overtook him. Was this Hell? Perhaps he was damned to an eternity of seeing things he knew he would never see again, longing for things he could never change.

He wished the mist clouding his vision would clear. This did not fit in with how he imagined Hell at all.

"Kerry, Come back to me, damn you!" There followed a few carefully chosen expletives he had never heard from Cat's lips before, and then his name, spoken again so softly and with such anguish it seemed to penetrate his very soul.

Through his painfully half opened eyes, her face wavered before him, as if seen through a badly calibrated tri-dee viewer. "Cat," he whispered with an effort, his throat so dry he could hardly speak. "You... are...alive."

Chapter Twenty-Two

The sense of relief that welled up inside her threatened to rob her of rational thought. For a moment Cat could only stare at him, mutely blinking away the treacherous tears of despair she'd allowed to fall when she feared there might be no hope for him.

"Yes," she whispered at last, allowing herself to breathe again. "Yes, and by some miracle, so are you." She withdrew her water flask from her pack and pressed it to his lips, urging him to take slow sips.

"Thanks." Kerry tried to raise himself on one elbow.

She put a hand behind his shoulder to help support him. "You sure you're strong enough to sit?"

"I will be…in a moment." After a minute or so, with her help, Kerry managed to sit, although his face showed the strain of his ordeal. To her amazement and relief, he appeared to have no physical injuries.

"I don't…quite…understand what is going on here." He raked a hand through his hair in the familiar gesture.

"Neither do I. One moment I was fighting with Shalina, the next I stood on the edge of the cliff with her and below us was what looked like the entrance to Hell. Then…" her voice trailed off.

He did not need to know about her encounter with the snakes. Not yet, anyway. After a moment, she continued, "Then I'm kneeling here beside you, and you look like death."

"For a while there, I thought I *was* dead," Kerry told her pragmatically. He clasped his hand to his head. "I have one hell of a headache."

She could not help a low chuckle, partly of relief and partly of amazement. How could he talk in this offhand, almost casual manner? He might almost be recovering after a rave at some interplanetary tavern, instead of a deadly bargain for their lives.

"Oh, if that's all you have, you should count yourself lucky. I thought the damage was much worse." *I thought I'd lost you.* "Thank you," she whispered, making sure he heard her now. "Thank you for not choosing to let me die, even to save your friends and your ship." She hesitated before adding even more softly, "But how do you think I could have lived with myself if they'd killed you?" *How could I live at all if you had died?*

She bit her lower lip. Did he know she'd heard him? Even when she and Shalina stood, completely immobile, unable to so much as blink, she still heard him negotiating for her life and those of his friends and crewmates.

"How could I do otherwise?" he asked, as if there had never been any alternative. "Here, help me to stand."

"I'm not sure you should. Perhaps you should rest a while."

"I will be fine." He reached out both his hands, and as she took them in hers, she felt a familiar tingle rush through her at his touch, heating her blood and threatening to rob her of reason. She took some of his weight as he stood a little unsteadily.

"You're sure you're all right?"

"Yes, I just need to sort my head out. Did what I think happened really happen, or was I hallucinating?"

"It depends on what you think happened," she said, trying to keep her voice from faltering as he released her hands.

"I saw you with Shalina on the edge of a precipice with a river of fire below."

"Yes, I remember fighting with Shalina," she said, wincing as she recalled the memory. "But then everything went hazy, as if I'd lost consciousness for a few moments. The next thing I remember is standing on the edge of a cliff, looking down at something that looked like the mouth of Hades, and hearing you bartering for our lives." She allowed the ghost of a smile to play about her lips. "I think we can safely say you were wrong about being 'bad luck' where women are concerned. I'm living proof that's not the case."

"Then what about Shalina?"

"You can't blame yourself for what happened. You tried to save her." Cat swallowed hard, trying to erase the memory of Shalina's screams from her mind. "I can't help wondering why they allowed her to…to die, and yet I was somehow saved from going over the edge."

"Perhaps they were aware of her crimes and it was their way of inflicting punishment."

"Then their methods are singularly cruel and brutal, don't you think?" A sudden thought entered her mind. "Do you think Jon would have seen what happened to Shalina?"

"I suspect it depends if the Therocians wanted him

to. I hope not. He knew her to be a traitor, and she betrayed his affection, but it would have been a difficult thing to see. Shalina may have had it coming, but I know how hard it is to watch someone you love die." His eyes softened as he studied her face. "I am sorry if I seem insensitive, I almost forgot she was your sister. It must have been just as hard for you—"

Cat half turned, to hide the pain of Shalina's betrayal. "I can't grieve for her now. Perhaps it will hit me later, but now I just feel numb. She changed so much from when we were children. She…just wasn't my sister any more. She would have killed me without a moment's regret." She sighed deeply before turning back to him. "Do you think he's still in love with her?"

"I believe his feelings changed when he discovered she was still alive and working for the Union. I think he cared for her up to that moment, though, despite everything."

He touched his communicator. "I need to find out if the others are all right, and if the *Destiny* is able to send a ferry down for us."

Once more, she watched his face register utter frustration as the instrument failed to make any connection with the *Destiny*. He shook his head. "I am sorry. I promised to get you off this planet and one way or another I will, if it is in my power to do so. Meanwhile, we will just have to hope the Therocians decide to stop playing games and restore our communication.

****

While they talked, the sky darkened. The shadows coalesced and became indistinct as the air shimmered and began to glow again. When the full light returned,

231

the landscape had changed once more.

Gone were the nondescript colours, the quicksand and strangely formed trees. In their place, tall, silvery buildings with spires and turrets reached into a pink, cloudless sky. Mosaic pavements and pathways, and elegant, stately houses arranged in an orderly, uncluttered fashion between avenues of trees. Small, graceful crafts zipped noiselessly thorough the air. Beings, similar to the Therocians who had stood in judgment over them, went about their daily business. Fountains tinkled in the square and the land around grew green and lush. Carpets of vivid, multi-coloured flowers, and tall, graceful trees bordered the walkways.

Kerry passed his hand across his face, wondering if his imagination was playing tricks, but when he glanced at Cat, her expression told him she was seeing the same things. A cloud of iridescent particles gradually materialized and formed into the figures present the first time they found themselves in the Therocians' "court room." The one who acted as spokesperson stepped forward and the others faded, and became indistinct, dancing like dust motes on the periphery of his vision.

"Now what?" he rasped out. "Surely you would not set any more trials for us? Haven't you already put us through enough?"

The Therocian who stood before them smiled benignly, almost like a parent regarding her wayward, but eager to please, children.

"No, no more trials. You passed the last one we set you, and we have kept our word and your ship and her crew are safe. We believe there may yet be hope for humankind. You were willing to sacrifice your own life to save those of your friends and the ship that is so important to you. We find this commendable." She turned toward Cat. "And the woman faced her greatest fear in order to come to your aid."

He glanced at Cat, an unspoken question on his lips, but she looked away, a faint blush colouring her cheek.

"You have exhibited something we did not believe the human race was capable of from our observations of your world, and those your species has conquered. Self-sacrifice for the survival of the majority."

"I am glad we have given you some amusement," he said, his voice loaded with sarcasm. "It is hardly the first time a man was willing to sacrifice his own life for the lives of his friends."

"Indeed, and twenty-three of your centuries ago, one man made that sacrifice for the whole of humanity. He was the only perfect example of the human species before or since. We have attempted to establish if you have learned anything from His sacrifice."

He shook his head, as he processed her words. "So all these 'trials' pitting us against each other—it *was* all for your amusement, you were playing some universal mind game?"

"You are incorrect in your assumptions. We do nothing for our own amusement. Did you not understand what we told you before? This planet guards the gateway to what you would term a wormhole, a portal into another dimension, far beyond your ability to comprehend. We are charged with safeguarding it, and maintaining its secrecy, until humankind is ready for its secrets to be revealed.

"You are the first of your species to reach this

sector of space. We wished to ascertain what you have learned throughout the centuries, and to try to educate you in the futility of violence. Your trials provided a way to test your intentions and ensure you posed no threat to this world and the wonders beyond. You did at least prove that there is some hope for your species, and some of you are able to rise above the avarice and selfishness that inflicts humanity like a terrible sickness. We are hopeful that, in time, your kind will be wise enough and mature enough to enter through the gateway."

When neither of them replied, she went on, "I see you still have many questions. We feel you have earned the right to at least a partial explanation and we are now prepared to answer some of your concerns."

"In that case," he said, "tell us—was everything we have been through an illusion, and are we still on the planet Robigo?"

"Yes, you are still on that planet. You are currently seeing an image of our home world, Therocia. That is also an illusion and a shadow of the reality of our natural domain. We came here with our ancestors millennia ago, and remained here as guardians and protectors, while they returned to Therocia."

"Then Robigo is not your original home planet?"

The entity turned to Cat. "No. As we said, we are merely guardians of what you would call a stargate."

Addressing Kerry, she went on, "To answer your question, the ways in which we tested you, the wild animals, the explosion and the air burst caused by a bolide entering the atmosphere, even the raid in the town, were all actual occurrences. The ravine in the last trial was also real, although we added some illusionary effects. On the other occasions we merely shifted locations and transported you to different areas of the planet, to see how you would react in certain situations."

"What about the other officials of the Union?" Kerry asked. If they were ever to get away from this planet and there was a possibility of the Union confronting the *Destiny* in deep space, he wanted to know. A thought occurred to him. "Did they really exist, or were they just images and memories plucked from our minds?"

"They seemed real enough when we fought them," Cat stated.

"Don't forget the gunfight with the ancient weapons from the American West," he reminded her, "if they could convince you that was real, why not other things as well? After all, we were shown visions conjured from our own memories."

"That vision of a period in your Earth history was, as you surmise, based on memories we found when we probed from your mind," the woman confirmed. "We created images of your antagonists in order to gauge your reactions when you were each seeing a different reality. The natives of this planet, however, actually exist, and you have encountered some of them. They are even more primitive than your species, and are completely unaware of us, the Therocians. The humans you call 'The Union' were also physically present. Sadly they represent all that is wrong with humankind and, until that element of your species changes its ways, humanity will never evolve enough to share in the wonders we could teach you."

"So what have you done with them?"

"They have been dealt with. Those who were deemed of sufficient humanity to be allowed to continue with their lives have returned to their mother ship. You need not concern yourselves with them. They will trouble you no further. All recollection of recent events and the location of this planet, and this sector of space, have been wiped from their memories."

"Why were our telepaths, Delian and Regin unable to read your thoughts and deduce what was really going on?"

"It was very easy to block our transmissions so the telepaths could not read them. It is a device their race use themselves to avoid the insanity that being open to thoughts from others and projecting their thoughts to other telepaths would bring. In the same way, we prevented your communications systems from working when it served our purpose."

"So now—are we free to go?"

The woman waved a dismissive hand, much as a person might swat away a troublesome insect. "Yes, go, we have had enough of your questions. Be aware that if you enter this zone again, the dangers you faced here will be as nothing to what will lie in store for you. Be sure to warn your companions and any of your species who might be tempted to explore this region.

"One more thing," he said, choosing his words with care. "Are you going to release our ship and restore our communications? And will you return us to our ship the same way you brought us here? Your species may be able to create illusions and teleport living beings at will. Ours requires something a little more substantial."

"Of course, you humans are still so very primitive.

But we have grown tired of this experiment. You already have the means to return to your ship." Before they could ask further questions, the Therocians winked out of sight as if they never existed.

****

For a moment, Kerry wondered if the Therocians were again playing tricks on them. They stood once more in the clearing where Cat had crashed her escape vessel. The Union hyperspeedster loomed before them, poised for take-off, and there was no sign of the Union ferry or any of the Union personnel.

They looked at each other, and he could not help smiling at the slightly bemused look on Cat's face.

"Well," she said at length, "whatever the Therocians say, I feel like I've been part of some cosmic experiment, like a laboratory specimen. At least they explained some of the anomalies we experienced—not the disappearance of the bodies of the men who were shooting at you when I first found you though."

"No, I suspect they caused them to dematerialize in order to confuse us. I can only assume they were natives of this planet who viewed us as hostile."

"Hmm—if the Therocians were trying to get us to doubt our own sanity, they certainly succeeded," Cat muttered.

A slight rustling in the undergrowth caused them to turn, weapons drawn. When one of the bushes moved and became the lithe form of Shifter, they both relaxed and looked back to the ship. Cat reached out to rub the chameleopard behind the ears as he nuzzled against her leg.

"There's our answer," Kerry said, indicating the

ship. "Now all we have to do is see if we can fly her, assuming I can find a way to gain entry." He scrutinized it from where they stood. "It will take me a little while to neutralize the shield. And once we're past the shield there is always the risk of a booby trap or two."

"I'll help with that. I know a bit about explosives. Let's get on with it and see if we can sniff them out, if there are any, and find a way of defusing them. I don't fancy being blown to kingdom come," Cat said, looking up from fondling Shifter, and grinning back.

He muttered, "Neither do I, if I can help it."

\*\*\*\*

"That should do it," Kerry said, as he replaced the last computer chip set into a recess in the hull. Cat drew her arm across her brow. The last couple of hours, when she and Kerry had worked together to disarm the anti-intrusion devices, were hard work. The explosive devices were fairly standard though. She'd worked on similar ones on board Union ships. She made no attempt to hide her admiration as Kerry made short work of reprogramming the access code to gain entry into the vehicle. She covered up a sigh. With her weaponry skills, and his computer knowledge and prowess, they could have made a formidable team.

The hatch slid back, and they stepped on board the ship.

Wherever or whoever Shalina and Dorian had stolen it from, she was certainly a beauty and more advanced than any Federation ship she'd come across. She seated herself in the pilot's seat and studied the control panel while Kerry checked there were no hidden anti-intruder devices on board. Shifter stretched out in the recreation area as if keeping watch.

Sometime later, Kerry looked up from analysing the computer systems. "The computer bio-system is nothing like as sophisticated as *Metisa*, of course, but adequate. Also, the ship has two ferries. I can use one to get back on board the *Destiny*, and then you can take over this ship. I am sure you have the connections to get her registered and transferred to your name—whichever one you decide to use." He paused and flashed a sardonic smile. "Provided you promise not to use her for 'privateering', of course."

She gave him a look.

"Think you'll be able to handle her? She is a big ship for a single pilot."

"Of course, the basic controls aren't that dissimilar to Union ships, and most of them are computer controlled anyway. I can't wait to fly this baby." She knew she should feel elated at the prospect of being in command of her own ship once more, but all she could think of was that once he left for the *Destiny*, she would never see him again. "Thank you," she said, averting her eyes and pretending to study the controls again. "And at least it means I'll be out of your hair at last."

Kerry raised an eyebrow in that questioning way she'd come to know so well.

"I'm not sure I would put it that way. We had some interesting times together."

"Yes, we did, didn't we?" She sighed inwardly.

It would to be hard to say goodbye. She'd been a loner for a long time, but somehow she'd become used to working alongside him and to having his companionship. *Face the truth. Your feelings go a lot deeper than that*. Once she knew the truth about Shalina and her treachery, her longstanding quest for retribution was no longer relevant, and the animosity between them lost its edge. It became almost a friendly rivalry. One, which for her had deepened into admiration and respect, and...*Yes, go on, admit it*...she had grown to love this man. A man she once hated enough to want to kill.

If only they'd met in a different time under other circumstances, things might have worked out very differently.

****

With Kerry's assistance, Cat programmed the computer to respond to her verbal commands. She also acquainted herself with the ship's controls until she was confident she could handle her in lift-off and flight. The ship would not be difficult to control, once she had the hang of it, and she could not deny it would be good to pilot her own ship again.

Lift off from Robigo went smoothly and once free of the planet's atmosphere, Cat breathed a sigh of relief. There were times when she'd thought they would never escape from the planet and the Therocians. She would not be sorry if she never saw this sector of space again. Reflecting on their final words to her and Kerry, there was clearly much more to this planet than its original bleak aspect would suggest. She had the feeling they'd trespassed on what amounted to "hallowed" ground, and the concept was mind-blowing.

They both took advantage of the sonic showers and after a change of clothing and a quick meal, made preparations for the transfer to the *Destiny*. Kerry made some calculations, and cross-referenced with the computer to ascertain the optimum window to launch the escape vessel. He seemed lost in his thoughts and said few words during the voyage out. She remained silent herself, reluctant to intrude or break his concentration, but could not hold back a gasp of admiration when the *Destiny* came into view on the external scanner. She adjusted the controls to bring it in closer. Although she knew she'd been on board the starship, since she was unconscious at the time, she'd had no opportunity to appreciate its size or beauty. Even at that distance, it was magnificent.

Kerry always spoke in glowing terms about the *Destiny* but nothing could prepare her for the spectacle the ship presented. She could understand now how he and the others felt about her. She swallowed a pang of envy, not just for this beautiful ship the crew thought of as home, but also for the obvious camaraderie between them. Androids could not compare with the friendship and loyalty of a human crew.

"I need to try to contact the ship again," Kerry said, interrupting her musings. "Always assuming the Therocians do not have any more surprises in store for us and are no longer blocking our transmissions."

Chapter Twenty-Three

Kerry finished adjusting the settings on the communications system. He waved his hand across the holo-receiver, and Jon's face appeared, flickered, and then faded momentarily before the image re-appeared and stabilized.

"Kerry. At last. According to *Metisa*, you're on board an unidentified alien ship. What's been going on? And is Cat with you?"

"It's a long story. And yes, Cat is here. The question is…what happened to you?"

"We've been on board the *Destiny*, waiting, as you requested, for you let us know when you wanted us to send down a ferry to Robigo."

"Waiting as *I* requested? I made no such request." Kerry half turned and shot a perplexed glance her way before continuing. "You have no idea what happened down there, have you?"

Cat peered over Kerry's shoulder. The rest of the crew stood behind Jon on the flight deck. The commander's expression changed to a frown as he consulted the data on a small screen beside him.

"I have the transcription of the message here. You said you had something you needed to discuss with Cat. The scanners showed you both on the surface. Then the screens went dead for several minutes before *Metisa* registered a ship launch from the surface. Did something happen I should know about?"

"It seems the Therocians were up to their tricks again. I will fill you in when I return to the *Destiny.*"

Did he mean he would tell Jon about Shalina? That would not be an easy conversation. Cat had difficulty coming to terms with the events of the last few hours herself. She had a feeling Kerry did not intend to tell Jon how he had been willing to sacrifice himself for her and Shalina, and for the *Destiny*'s crew.

"About the Therocians," Jon said, "*Metisa* made a comprehensive scan of the planet and came up with a substantial amount of data. You will need to go through it thoroughly when you're back on board the *Destiny*, but I've re-run the data myself, several times, and the conclusion is—well—astounding. *Metisa* detected a colossal energy signature, consistent with a gigantic artificial intelligence—apparently, some sort of collective AI, in fact. It appeared to emanate from several kilometres beneath the surface of the planet."

Kerry glanced back at her, and the expression on his face indicated this information was not entirely unexpected.

"I've been mulling that idea over myself. Some of the readings on my instruments made no sense, but I put it down to what we assumed were solar flares. If we are right, it seems safe to assume the Therocians themselves were never on this planet at all, not in any physical sense, anyway. It is likely their images were projected by the 'collective' itself." He paused to let the information sink in. "The implications are astounding. Not only could this Intelligence transmit living matter to various parts of the planet, and through space itself, it was able to probe our deepest memories and create illusions that had actual, physical consequences. It seems our human adversaries were real enough, as were the injuries we sustained." His voice was cynical as he commented, "We've been played like pawns in a virtual game of chess."

"More than a game though," Cat said. "According to what we were told, we seem to have stood trial for the entire human race. The Therocians…" she hesitated a moment, "I suppose we should refer to them as the 'AI collective', not only did they have the ability to make us react to different scenarios in some sort of virtual reality, they, or it, basically threatened to annihilate the entire human race if we failed to achieve the standards it set."

"And judging by its corporate ability to inflict instant pain and death, it might actually possess the means to do so," Kerry added. "Apparently, this planet is some sort of stargate, and the AI is determined to protect it by every means at its disposal. It, or they, indicated it would be impossible for us to comprehend whatever lay beyond, and that the human race has a long way to go before we will be allowed access to its secrets." He paused, while the crew on board the *Destiny* registered varying expressions of amazement. "We were also warned of severe retribution to any ships that enter this sector of space again. We should be grateful that they decided to 'put us on trial' to calculate the possibility of the human species achieving the standard this intelligence requires of us, rather than just blasting us out of the ether."

There was a long pause before Jon replied, "That is a lot to process. We need to discuss all this further when you're back on board. We're maintaining fixed orbit around the planet, and I assume you'll need to make some computer calculations before you can give us your ETA."

"I've already made preliminary calculations, and bearing in mind your orbital position, I intend to transfer to one of this ship's ferries and reach the *Destiny* in…" Kerry glanced at the instrument on his wrist, "two hours and forty-seven minutes. I will contact you again from the ferry as soon as I've launched."

"Cat isn't coming with you?"

"No. She will take this ship. It was the one—" He hesitated, and for a moment Cat thought he was about to say "the one Shalina used." Instead, he said, "The one the Union left behind."

"I see. You're quite happy to fly the ship alone, Cat?" Jon's tone softened, as if he wondered if this was really her decision.

"Absolutely," she assured him, forcing a smile. "She's well set up, and once Kerry confirms he's safely transferred to your ship, I can be on my way too."

"You're sure you don't want to come with us? You're welcome to join the crew. I've discussed it with the others here, and we think you'd fit in on the *Destiny* just fine."

She shook her head. "Thank you. I appreciate the offer, but I guess I'll just see where this beauty will take me."

Jon may have discussed her staying with the rest of the crew, but he hadn't discussed it with Kerry, and Kerry had not asked her to stay. If he had any feelings for her, he would surely have already asked her to go with him to the *Destiny*, rather than suggesting she take the Union hyperspeedster. She could hardly admit she could not face the idea of seeing him every day, knowing she could never be anything more to him than a pleasant diversion. Sooner or later, she'd give herself away and reveal her feelings for him, and that would make life difficult for everyone.

"Travel in safety, then. The offer stands, if you should change your mind."

"Thank you—all of you," she said, nodding to the rest of the crew. She turned away, afraid her face would betray her, and aware of how much she would miss them all even though she'd known them for only a relatively short time.

She turned back to a darkened com-screen and watched as Kerry checked a mass of data. She waited in silence while he finished the calculations and made some adjustments.

"Everything is working as it should. I don't foresee any problems. This ship will take you wherever you want to go"

"Thanks." There was so much she wanted to say, but somehow the words would not come. "I suppose you'll be leaving soon?"

"There really seems no reason to delay my return any longer. Once I leave, you can program in your projected trajectory and go…wherever you intend to go. I can adjust the ferry's speed and trajectory to ensure successful rendezvous with the *Destiny* within the projected window.

"Of course." He could have safely waited until the ship was much closer to the *Destiny* before launching the ferry. However, he seemed to have decided they'd said everything they needed to say to each other, and it was obvious he could not wait to get away from her.

"I'll come with you to the launch bay."

Kerry made no reply, and together they took the turbo-lift to the launch area, in silence. She would give a lot to know what went on in his mind at that moment, but it somehow felt like an invasion of privacy to ask him.

Kerry reached for the control to open the inner airlock door where transit Ferry One awaited him, but did not activate it. Instead, he turned to face her. "It seems this is goodbye then."

"I suppose it is," she said, trying to avoid a catch in her voice. "I'll miss trying to shoot you."

"Yes. I have to say I'm rather glad we did not succeed in killing each other. Perhaps we will meet again, in another time…another galaxy."

They exchanged glances. Once again it seemed almost as if he'd read her mind and tapped into her earlier thoughts.

They were probably both thinking the same thing now. The chance of them ever seeing each other again, in the vastness of space, was highly unlikely. It would have taken only a few words from Kerry for her to accept Jon's offer and leave this ship behind, to go with him to join the crew of the *Destiny* and swear to be at his side forever, whatever befell them. But he was immersed in the past, still in love with a memory, and she could not compete with a ghost.

He smiled his devastating smile, and her heart lurched painfully. That smile would stay with her for the rest of her life.

They held each other's gaze for a long while. A handshake seemed too formal after all they'd endured together. A hug, which surely they both knew would turn into an embrace, was too intimate for two people who would never meet again.

"Contact me as soon as you reach the *Destiny,*" Cat said at last. "I'll keep her on minimum sub-light drive until I hear from you."

"Of course." He paused for a moment. "Take care of yourself—and the wolf."

"You, too." She tore her gaze away from his, and with the chameleopard at her heels, turned to walk the dozen or so steps to the turbo-lift. She could watch the launch of the ferry from the flight deck.

As she reached it, she paused and listened for the whine of the airlock activating, needing to know when he left, but not wanting to look round and find herself alone.

Instead, a single word broke the silence.

"*Cat.*"

\*\*\*\*

Kerry again raised his hand to activate the airlock control. A deep despondency descended over him like a cloak. Why was he hesitating? Stupid question. The answer was obvious. It had taken all his willpower not to take her in his arms and beg her to come back with him to the *Destiny*. What stopped him? His pride? His fear of rejection if he'd misjudged the situation and she felt nothing for him, after all?

For a while, he'd thought perhaps there really was something between them now, something that went deeper than the obvious chemistry. Despite their initial mutual distrust, they'd faced danger and hardship together, bared their souls to each other and faced trial by a force of immense, seemingly unlimited power.

After he'd nearly been killed by them, and Cat found him, he almost believed there could be a future for them, together. Yet she seemed to have become distant since they'd been on board this ship, withdrawn almost, and when Jon asked her to join them, she'd refused. Surely, if she cared anything for him she would have accepted Jon's invitation in a heartbeat?

He listened to her footsteps as she approached the turbo lift. The melancholy turned to something approaching desperation. He was about to let the only woman who'd meant anything to him since Jess walk out of his life—the one woman with whom he could imagine a future.

He turned and called her name.

\*\*\*\*

One word, hanging in the air. Her name, spoken low. One word, but it was enough to make her catch her breath and swing round.

The familiar rich timbre of his voice, and even more than that, the inflection as he spoke her name, sent shockwaves through her body. His hypnotic gaze drew her toward him. He crossed the space between them, and the next moment his arms enfolded her as she melted into his embrace. His lips burned hers in a kiss, deep and slow at first, then fiercely passionate, as if he was consumed with a hunger only she could quell. She entwined her arms around his neck and pressed even closer to him. Her lips parted, and his tongue teased and danced with her own, sending shivers of desire through every nerve. He gave a deep sigh and broke the kiss. He looked deep into her eyes, his own no longer cold, the pain replaced by a softness she'd never seen there before.

"Cat, I have come to realize…you mean more to me than I could ever have imagined. You fill a void in my life—something I did not think could ever be filled. Did you really want us to go our separate ways?"

She shook her head and clung to him, moulding the curves of her body to his, holding him so tightly she found it hard to breathe. "Of course not…but there's no way I could accept being…second best."

He ran the back of his fingers along her cheek and down to trace the curve of her lips.

"You could never be 'second best'." His lips claimed hers again in a kiss that made her want to hold him like this forever, and never let him go. This time there was no holding back for either of them. The sparks that had smouldered between them for so long ignited into full-blown flames. He deepened the kiss, and she moaned deep in her throat. Her blood coursed through her veins like quicksilver, and raw desire threatened to rob her of all self-control. Holding her close, one hand cradling the back of her head, the other against the small of her back, he pressed her body even closer to his own. She felt his arousal, his desire, and her heart pounded in her chest like a trapped bird trying to escape.

Time seemed to stand still, and when at last Kerry ended the kiss, she felt a sharp sense of loss as she had after the first time he'd kissed her on Robigo. He brushed his lips down the side of her neck then touched them to her mouth once more before pressing them to her brow. He held her slightly away from him and gazed into her eyes as if trying to read into her soul.

"I never thought I'd say this, or that I could ever feel anything for another woman—but I love you. I *love* you, Cat Kincaid." With his free hand, he loosened the scarf she wore at the nape of her neck, and ran his fingers slowly through her hair as it swept around her shoulders. "Jess would not have wanted me to mourn all my life. It took me a long time to realize that. She taught me how to love, and I will never forget her—"

"I wouldn't want you to," she whispered.

"But she is my past," he continued, "and I believe it is time to lay the past to rest and look to the future." He took a deep breath. "I need you in my future. Do you think there can be one for two mismatched people like us? Do you think we could go beyond a week without trying to kill each other?"

She could not repress a mischievous smile. "As I recall, it was always more me trying to kill you, and you'll never know how glad I am I didn't. I never imagined I could ever fall in love with you," she whispered, "but I did." Heat flooded her body, her heart thudded against her ribs, and she who now feared nothing except losing him, trembled as if afraid.

He placed his fingers beneath her chin and raised her face once more to his, obliging her to look again into his eyes until it seemed she might drown in their depths. "You have not answered my question."

"We made it this far," she whispered. "I think perhaps there's a chance we could make it work."

He regarded her with a tenderness that made her almost lose control. "Then let me stay here with you. Jon and the others will understand."

She slowly shook her head.

Kerry's eyes flashed, and for a moment, the pain returned. "Why, Cat? If you love me, why not?"

"Because you belong with the *Destiny*. She's your

ship, your dream, and I love you too much to ask you to leave her."

"She's just a ship, Cat. Metal, electronics, and bio-components. That is all. Yes, she is the culmination of all my research and endeavours, everything Jon and I worked for, but if it comes to a choice, I can't lose you. I *won't* lose you. Not now. Not if I know you care for me." He kissed her brow. "If you won't take me with you, then reconsider your decision and come with me, to the *Destiny.*"

Relief flooded through her, and she ran her fingers across his lips. "You only had to ask. I thought—I thought you didn't care enough to ask me yourself. I never wanted to leave you."

He closed his eyes for a moment, and sighed deeply. "Then promise me you never will."

"Never. You're stuck with me now." She glanced down at the animal beside her and added, "But you do realize if you take me, you have to take Shifter as well?"

"I would not expect anything else," he said, with that rare, flashing smile.

"What about this ship though? She's a beauty, we can't just abandon her."

"No problem, once we're on board the *Destiny* again, we can send out a tractor beam to tow her, until we decide what to do with her."

He drew her close again and brought his mouth down hard on her own. Again, his tongue caressed hers, and she uttered a soft moan. She slid her hand beneath his shirt, running it over his skin. Her breasts ached with the desire to press them against his bare chest, to feel his skin against hers. She began to unfasten his tunic, her longing for him almost unbearable.

"Perhaps we should wait to continue this…conversation until we are on board the *Destiny*," he whispered, halting the progress of her fingers by taking both her hands in his own. He kissed the back of each one in turn. "As much as I want to make love to you, this is hardly the best place—"

"Why do we have to wait?" she asked softly. "There's no hurry to launch a ferry now we're not going our separate ways. We can wait until we're closer to the *Destiny*. I had a look around the ship while you were busy configuring the communications system. There are a couple of very comfortable cabins on this level, and we have a little time to kill."

**\*\*\*\***

Cat sent a mental message of thanks to whoever designed this ship, for having the foresight to arrange for cabins on the same level as the launch area. Even better, the access codes were set to zero. So they did not have to waste time decrypting it.

Kerry gave a swift, verbal command to the computer to alert them in good time to launch the ferry when they were at optimum proximity to the *Destiny*.

"Now," Kerry said softly, drawing her close and pressing another kiss on her lips. "Where were we?"

She chuckled and twined one arm around his neck. With her other hand she unfastened his shirt, while he performed the same service for her. She lifted her arms so he could slip her tunic over her head and let it drop to the floor at her feet. Next, he slipped the straps of her silky undergarment down her arms and unfastened it, to send it to join the tunic. She nestled against his skin revelling in the feel of him, his warmth and his musky, masculine scent. She gave a soft moan, the sound almost a purr, as his fingers travelled slowly over her breasts. Spasms of desire shot through her when he cupped each one in turn and pressed a kiss to it before turning his attention back to her lips. She could no more stop her body from responding to his than she could prevent the blood from coursing through her veins. Nor could the passion, simmering for so long, be prevented from igniting, finally allowing the flames to consume them both.

She unbuckled the belt from around his waist, and he lifted her to the bunk, swiftly removed her remaining garments, and then his own. Their hands explored and fondled each other's warm, naked skin. She trembled as Kerry's mouth swept down her neck and feathered kisses along the swell of her breasts. His lips fastened on one nipple, kissing and teasing with his tongue, and caused her to groan with desire. He paid attention to the other breast, sucking the erect nipple gently and circling with his tongue, before his lips travelled further down her body, kissing, caressing, teasing.

"Please," she gasped, "don't make me wait. I need you. I want you—now."

Every touch was sweet torture. The warmth of his body against her skin nearly drove her to a fever pitch. She felt a quiver run through him and knew he wanted her just as much, but he seemed determined not to hurry. She ran her fingers over his body, caressing whatever parts of him she could reach.

"Hush, my love. Have patience. I want our first time to be something to be savoured." He eased her down on the sheets, and covered her body with his.

His fingers found her most sensitive place, and she

moaned even louder, but he had no mercy until she trembled on the brink of climax. She arched her back to meet him, and when she thought she could not bear to wait another moment, he thrust deep inside her. Her arms around his shoulders gripped harder. Pushing herself against him, she demanded his whole length, wanting to merge completely—body, heart, and soul— until they were truly one.

He gave a deep growl of satisfaction, as she responded, and they rose and fell together in perfect harmony, their passion growing stronger and more urgent with each movement of their bodies.

A mounting glow of pleasure started somewhere deep within her until it grew almost unbearable, and finally, she cried out again and again. The joyous sensation increased in its intensity, and she lost all control. As she climaxed, the joy of his release exploded in time with her own, and he called out her name. Her whole body rocked with violent spasms of ecstasy until she thought she could stand the overwhelming waves of pleasure no more, and again an involuntary cry wrenched from her throat, as the universe exploded around her.

When they fell back, exhausted, he kissed her once more, and they lay together, limbs entwined, fingers clasped, exhausted in the afterglow, without the need for words.

Once she could breathe again, she turned in his arms and pressed her lips to his. "Is this what you meant when you said we'd probably kill each other in a week?" she asked coquettishly, as she rolled on top of him and ran her fingers through his hair.

He laughed softly, the sound re-awakening pulses

of desire along her nerve endings.

"Not exactly, but now you mention it, offhand, I could not think of a more pleasurable way to leave this life."

"But not yet," she said with a mischievous smile, holding him close. "Not for a long, long time yet."

Thank you for purchasing
this publication of The Wild Rose Press, Inc.

If you enjoyed the story, we would appreciate your
letting others know by leaving a review.

For other wonderful stories,
please visit our on-line bookstore at
www.thewildrosepress.com.

For questions or more information
contact us at
info@thewildrosepress.com.

The Wild Rose Press, Inc.
www.thewildrosepress.com

Stay current with The Wild Rose Press, Inc.

Like us on Facebook

https://www.facebook.com/TheWildRosePress

And Follow us on Twitter
https://twitter.com/WildRosePress